Holly Webb's
Kitten Tales

Illustrated by Sophy Williams

Other titles by Holly Webb

The Snow Bear

The Reindeer Girl

The Winter Wolf

Animal Stories:

Lost in the Snow

Alfie all Alone

Lost in the Storm

Sam the Stolen Puppy

Max the Missing Puppy

Sky the Unwanted Kitten

Timmy in Trouble

Ginger the Stray Kitten

Harry the Homeless Puppy

Buttons the Runaway Puppy

Alone in the Night

Ellie the Homesick Puppy

Jess the Lonely Puppy

Misty the Abandoned Kitten

Oscar's Lonely Christmas

Lucy the Poorly Puppy

Smudge the Stolen Kitten

The Rescued Puppy

The Kitten Nobody Wanted

The Lost Puppy

The Frightened Kitten

The Secret Puppy

The Abandoned Puppy

The Missing Kitten

The Puppy Who was Left Behind

The Kidnapped Kitten

The Scruffy Puppy

The Brave Kitten

The Forgotten Puppy

The Secret Kitten

A Home for Molly

My Naughty Little Puppy:

A Home for Rascal

New Tricks for Rascal

Playtime for Rascal

Rascal's Sleepover Fun

Rascal's Seaside Adventure

Rascal's Festive Fun

Rascal the Star

Rascal and the Wedding

Contents

www.hollywebbanimalstories.com

STRIPES PUBLISHING
An imprint of Little Tiger Press
1 The Coda Centre, 189 Munster Road,
London SW6 6AW

A paperback original
First published in Great Britain in 2014

ISBN: 978-1-84715-447-7

Sky the Unwanted Kitten

For Lucy

Chapter One

As the car started, Lucy pressed her face up against the window, staring sadly back at her home. Except it wasn't her home any more. In a few hours' time another family would arrive, and another removal lorry, just like the one that was lumbering down the road in front of her parents' car. She blinked back tears as they pulled away, staring back at Nutmeg and Ginger, the two friendly cats from the house next door. They'd been frightened away by all the fuss and bother of the removal men, but now they were back on their usual spot, the wall between Lucy's garden and the one next door. They liked to sunbathe on the bricks, and Lucy loved to play with them and cuddle them and pretend they were hers. She longed to have a cat of her own. She had asked her parents so many times, but they always said she would have to wait until she was older.

The ginger cats stared curiously after the car. Lucy rolled down her window and waved to them. Nutmeg mewed, and walked down the wall towards the street. Lucy sniffed miserably.

She couldn't believe she would never see them again. A few seconds later the car turned out of her road and she could no longer see the cats, or even the house.

"How long till we get there?" Kieran, Lucy's older brother, asked, unplugging his new iPod for a moment.

"A couple of hours, probably," their mum said. "We should definitely be settling in by lunchtime!"

"Doesn't it feel great, being on our way to our new home!" their dad added enthusiastically.

Lucy sniffed and said nothing. She clutched Stripy, her old toy cat, even tighter. They'd just left her home behind. What they were going to was only a horrible *house*. It would never, ever be home.

Lucy hardly spoke the whole journey. She just gazed out of the window, and worried to herself. A new house. A new school. No friends! She missed Ellie,

10

her best friend, loads already. Ellie would be in the middle of PE right now. *I wonder if she's missing me too?* Lucy thought.

"We're almost there!" her mum said excitedly, jerking Lucy out of her daydream, where she was back at school playing football with Ellie. "Look, Lucy, this is our street! Doesn't it look lovely?"

Lucy made a small *mmm* sort of noise. It was nice. Pretty gardens and friendly-looking houses. But it wasn't home.

"Oh good, the removal men are here already! Let's start getting unpacked. I bet you two want to see your rooms, don't you?" Dad sounded even more enthusiastic than Mum, if that was possible.

Lucy's new room was huge – much bigger than her old one, as Mum had happily pointed out. "And you can have it any colour you like, Lucy," she promised, placing a box of toys on the floor. "Maybe purple, what do you think?"

Lucy sat on the bed that the removal men had dumped in the corner, and gazed around, hugging Stripy. She was trying to be happy, but it was all so different.

The weekend flew past in a messy, grubby whirl of unpacking. Lucy felt left out – Mum and Dad were so happy about the move, and even Kieran was excited about the new house. She seemed to be the only one who missed home.

Now the moment she was really dreading had arrived – her first day at her new school. Surely someone who'd just moved ought to get at least a week off school, not just one Friday, spent driving to the new house. Even Kieran had complained that it wasn't fair they had to start their new schools today. Lucy trailed slowly across the empty playground after her mum, who was heading for the school office.

"Look, a school garden!" Mum said brightly. "And the sign says they have a gardening club. You'd love that, helping to plant seeds, wouldn't you?"

"Maybe," Lucy murmured. She saw a notice up about a football team, too, but there was no way she'd be able to join a team now, in the middle of term. *Everyone will already have their friends, and their gangs,* she thought unhappily. *I'm going to be so left out.*

The school secretary buzzed them in and took them over to Lucy's classroom. The school was actually much newer and smarter than the one Lucy had been going to until three days before, but she wished she was back at her scruffy old school. She stayed silent as her mum and the secretary chatted about the new computer suite. Her mouth was drooping sadly as they arrived at class 5W, and the secretary showed them in.

14

Her new teacher, Mrs Walker, smiled kindly at her, then announced, "Class, I'd like you to meet Lucy. She's just moved here, and I want you all to make her feel very welcome."

Lucy blushed and didn't know where to look. She hated everyone staring at her. Mrs Walker then took Lucy to one side, and said the class had really been looking forward to having her and she knew Lucy would be very happy once she'd settled in.

Lucy wasn't sure how she was supposed to do that – she'd never had to settle in anywhere before. She'd been to the same school since nursery, and she had known *everyone*.

"You sit here, Lucy, and Orla and Katie will look after you," Mrs Walker said. "You'll show Lucy where everything is, won't you, girls?"

Orla and Katie nodded and smiled. "Hi, Lucy!" they chorused.

"Hello," Lucy muttered, and sat

down as quickly as she could.

Orla and Katie tried their best, but Lucy was too shy to give more than yes or no answers to their polite questions. Eventually they gave up, and although they stayed with her all through the lunch hour, they stopped bothering to talk to her. *They don't like me*, Lucy told herself unhappily, as she listened silently to Orla telling Katie all about her ballet exam. *No one's even talking to me.*

Class 5W were actually quite a friendly group, but they couldn't do much faced with a silent Lucy, and she was so unhappy that she couldn't see that she needed to make an effort, too. Lucy was in the cloakroom putting on her coat to go home, when she heard some of the girls talking about her. She stayed frozen where she was, hidden behind a coat-rack, and listened.

"That new girl is a bit strange," someone said, giggling.

"Yeah, she hardly said a word all day." Lucy recognized the voice of Orla, one of her minders. "I hope Mrs Walker doesn't make us look after her tomorrow as well."

"Perhaps she thinks she's too good for us," another voice suggested. "I'm glad I didn't have to talk to her."

"Yeah, she does seem a bit stuck-up," Orla agreed.

Another girl from Lucy's class who was on the same side of the cloakroom as her gave Lucy a worried look, and coughed loudly. There was a sudden silence, then Orla's head popped round the coats, and her eyes went saucer-wide. She shot back again, and there was a burst of embarrassed giggling.

Lucy stood up and stalked out, blinking back tears. So what if they didn't like her? She certainly didn't like *them*. She heard the girls start whispering very fast, worrying about her telling Mrs Walker what they'd said. *I hate this school*, she thought, as she brushed her sleeve across her face angrily, trying to pretend to herself and everybody else that she wasn't crying.

"So how was your first day? Did you have a good time?" her mum asked eagerly as she met Lucy at the school gate.

"No. It was horrible, and I want to go home."

"Oh, Lucy, I'm sorry." Her mum looked at her anxiously. "I'm sure it'll get better, honestly. You just need to take a few days to get used to everything." She sighed, and then said in a cheerful voice, "I thought we'd walk back, it's not far. Kieran wanted to go by himself, so you and I can see if we spot any nice parks on the way home."

"Not there, *home*. I want to go back to our old house, and my proper school. I hate it here! No one likes me!" Lucy wailed. "I miss Ellie, and all my friends!"

Mum sighed again. "Lucy, your dad and I have explained this. We had to move. Dad's job is here now, and if we lived in our old house, he'd have to spend hours getting to work. We'd never see him. You wouldn't like that, would you?"

Lucy shook her head, and sniffed, trying not to cry where loads of people from school would see her. "I know," she whispered. "But it's really horrible here."

Her mum put an arm around her shoulder. "I know it's hard, sweetheart. But I promise it *will* get better. We'll just have to do lots of fun things to cheer you up."

Lucy rubbed her sleeve across her eyes. She couldn't believe she had to go back tomorrow.

Chapter Two

Lucy stared out of the classroom window, trying not to catch anyone's eye. She'd been at her new school for nearly a week now, but she still hadn't settled in. She couldn't forget the way Orla had talked about her. The awful thing was, Lucy knew she probably had seemed stuck-up and unfriendly, and all those things Orla had said. But it still seemed unfair. Didn't they know how lonely she was? Couldn't they see how difficult it was being the new girl? *At least it's Friday*, Lucy thought.

"Hey! Pssst…"

Lucy jumped slightly as someone prodded her hand. She looked up, confused. The pretty red-haired girl who sat across the table from her in her maths group had poked her with a pencil.

"Mrs Walker's watching you," the red-haired girl whispered. "If you weren't new, she'd have had a go at you by now. You've been looking out of the window for ages and we're supposed to be drawing that hexagon shape. Are you stuck? Do you need a rubber or something?"

Lucy shook her head, and gave her a tiny smile. "I'm OK, thanks," she whispered back, glancing quickly over at Mrs Walker. It was true – the teacher was looking her way. She bent her head over her book, suddenly feeling a little less miserable. Maybe there were some nice people in her new class after all.

When the bell rang for break, Lucy watched as the red-haired girl wandered out of the classroom with a group of other girls, all chatting excitedly. Maybe she should say something to her? But that would mean going up to her in front of the whole group. She would have to try to say something interesting, or just hang around on the edge of the circle until someone noticed her. She couldn't face that, what if they all ignored her? Lucy gave a little shudder and stayed put. She'd go to the school library. Like she had every other day this week.

The next morning, Lucy lay in bed, hugging Stripy, and feeling grateful that she didn't have to drag herself out to get ready for school. She'd tried to go back to sleep, but it wasn't working. She sighed, and looked round her room. So far she hadn't even bothered to unpack all her boxes. She was still hoping that somehow things would change and they could go home, but the hope was draining away with every day they stayed.

Kieran wasn't helping, either. He was loving his new school, and last night he'd spent most of dinner time talking enthusiastically about going to play football with some really cool new mates he'd made already. Mum was really excited about all the decorating that needed doing, and Dad had started his new job… Only Lucy was desperate to go back to their old home.

"Lucy! Hey!" It was Kieran, banging on her door.

Lucy ignored him, but he didn't go away. "Lucy! Get up, lazy!" He opened her door a crack, and peered in.

Lucy sat up. "Out! You're not allowed in my room!"

"OK, OK! But get up. Mum and Dad have got a surprise for you in the kitchen. You're going to love it!" he called, then thumped off back downstairs again.

A surprise! For a tiny moment Lucy's heart leaped. They were going home after all! She jumped out of bed and raced down after Kieran.

"Are we going home?" she gasped excitedly, catching him just at the bottom of the stairs.

Kieran gave her a strange look. "Of course not, silly, this *is* home now."

Lucy's shoulders slumped again. She trailed into the kitchen after him.

"Lucy!" Her parents were smiling happily at her, which just made Lucy feel more alone than ever.

"We've got a surprise for you, darling. Remember we said you'd have a special treat when we got here?" Mum pointed to a large box on the kitchen table.

Lucy stared dully at it. When her parents told them about the move, they'd said they would get Kieran an iPod, and that they had a special present in mind for Lucy, too. She'd been so sad missing everyone at home that she'd forgotten all about it.

She stared at the box, feeling just the tiniest bit excited. What could be inside? Suddenly the box started squeaking.

Lucy moved closer, curious despite herself. She opened the top flaps, which were attached together to make a sort of handle, and peered in.

Inside the box was the most beautiful creature Lucy had ever seen. A kitten with soft creamy fur, huge blue eyes, a chocolate-brown nose and gorgeously oversized brown ears.

Lucy gasped. A kitten!

The kitten looked anxiously up as the box opened, and mewed. It was a strange noise, almost like a baby crying, and Lucy immediately wanted to pick up the kitten and cuddle it. The kitten seemed to think this was a good idea, too. It stood up, balancing its paws on the side of the box, and shyly put its head over the side, looking up at Lucy with its amazing sapphire-blue eyes. "Wowl?" it asked pleadingly. "Wowl!"

Lucy lifted out the kitten, and it immediately snuggled into her pyjama top and started to purr. "Hello, little one," she said softly.

"Told you she'd love her," Lucy's dad said happily to her mum. "She's called Sky, Lucy. She's a Siamese. We know you've wanted a kitten for so long, and we think you're old enough now to look after a cat properly."

"Yes," said Mum. "We know how upset you've been about us moving to Fairford. But you can't be miserable with a beautiful kitten to play with, can you?"

Lucy stared at them in disbelief. The kitten was gorgeous, but it was as if her parents thought having a pet would suddenly make everything all right again. Lucy would forget about Ellie and all her friends, her school, her lovely old bedroom, and be happy for ever. Her eyes filled with angry, disappointed tears.

She carefully detached the kitten's tiny, needle-sharp claws from her pyjamas, and put her back in the box. Then she ran out of the kitchen, her shoulders heaving.

"Lucy!" Mum called after her, her voice shocked.

"Hey, Lucy, what's the matter?" Kieran said. "Mum, Dad, can I pick the kitten up? It's really cute, and it's crying."

Dad's voice was worried as he answered. "Yes, give her a cuddle, Kieran. I need to go and talk to Lucy, and find out what's wrong. I just don't understand, I was sure she'd be so happy."

Chapter Three

Lucy's dad had picked up Sky from the breeder early that morning. Sky had only left home before to go to the vets, and she'd always returned to her familiar room, and the big basket she shared with her mum and her brothers and sisters. Today she'd had to stay in the dark box on her own for ages, and she was so lonely. She wished she could go home, and snuggle up and let her mum lick her fur to make her feel better.

Where was she? It didn't smell like the vets, and it certainly wasn't home. She couldn't hear any other cats, either. She had started to cry for her home and her mum, and then someone had opened the box.

Sky shrank back into the corner of the box and peered up at the girl, feeling scared. Who was this? It wasn't one of the people she had met before. But then the girl, Lucy, had picked her up, and Sky had relaxed a little. She could see the delight in the girl's eyes, hear it in her quickened breathing, and feel it in the thud of her heart as the girl held her close. She had nestled snugly up against her, purring gratefully. She liked this person. The girl had stroked her, and nuzzled her ears, and rubbed her lovingly under her chin. But then suddenly she had taken her firmly round the middle, and put her back into that dark box.

Sky didn't understand. She had *felt* how happy the girl was to hold her. Lucy had been full of love, she knew it. So why had she suddenly changed her mind? The soft, cuddly person had turned stiff and cross, and Sky didn't know why.

Now she was sitting in a large, comfortable basket in the corner of the kitchen, with a bowl of kitten food and another bowl of water. There was a litter tray close by. She had everything she needed. But no one was with her, and she was so lonely. What had she done wrong? When Lucy had ran out, the boy had cuddled her briefly, then everyone had disappeared, and the kitchen was empty.

Sky was not used to being on her own. Until early this morning, she had lived in a house that was full of cats – her mum, and all her mum's sisters and their kittens, and her own sisters and brothers. There was a whole room full of boxes and big scratching posts and toys. Sky had spent most of her time with her mum, snuggling up in their basket, but she enjoyed being petted and stroked by people as well.

She wouldn't have minded leaving her home so much if Lucy had stayed cuddling her, but now she was alone she felt desperate to go back. She howled her loud, piercing Siamese howl, crying for someone to come and love her.

Upstairs in her room, Lucy could hear Sky. The kitten's sad, lonely wails made her want to cry, too. She knew exactly how Sky felt – taken away from her lovely home, and brought somewhere she didn't belong. She wished she could go and comfort her, but she just couldn't do it.

Lucy could hear her parents coming up the stairs, talking in low, worried voices, and she knew she had to explain how she was feeling. The trouble was she wasn't sure she *could*. Maybe it would be easier just to say she'd changed her mind about wanting a cat?

Her parents came in, and sat next to her on her bed. Her mum put an arm round her, but Lucy sat stiff and tense.

"I'm sorry, but I don't want a kitten," she said tiredly when Dad asked what was wrong.

Her parents exchanged confused glances. "But Lucy, you've begged for one for years!" Mum protested. "Every Christmas and birthday, a kitten's been top of your list. Now we've finally moved to a house big enough to have a cat, and on a nice quiet road, and you've changed your mind!"

"Yes, I've changed my mind," Lucy echoed.

"We thought you'd love a kitten," Dad said, shaking his head. "I just don't understand. All that time you used to spend playing with Nutmeg and Ginger next door. Mrs Jones used to joke that they were more your cats than hers."

Lucy's eyes filled with tears again at the thought of Nutmeg and Ginger. She missed them so much.

There was another mournful cry from downstairs. "That poor kitten," Mum said. "She doesn't know what's going on. We'd better go down so she isn't all on her own. Lucy, I know you're missing our old home, but we thought Sky would cheer you up. She really needs someone to look after her."

Lucy didn't answer, and kept her eyes fixed firmly on the floor. She knew that! She was desperate to go and cuddle Sky, and tell her everything would be all right. But things weren't all right, and it was no use pretending.

Lucy glanced up as her parents shut the door. As soon as she was sure that they were both at least halfway down the stairs, she buried her head in her pillow and cried and cried. A kitten! At last! And she couldn't keep her!

Eventually, Lucy dragged herself up from her bed. She wanted someone to talk to – she wanted Ellie! Lucy took out a pen and her favourite cat writing paper from one of the boxes, and started to write to her about everything.

Hi Ellie!

Mum and Dad have just given me a gorgeous Siamese kitten - she's so cute and soft to cuddle, and she's got the biggest blue eyes you've ever seen. I should be really happy, but the thing is I can't keep her! They think giving me a kitten will make me cheer up, and not miss home and you and all my friends. Mum even said so! Well, that's not going to happen.

Lucy started to cry again, and her tears smudged the ink on the page. She scrunched up the unfinished letter and threw it in the bin. It was just so unfair! A beautiful kitten, just like she

43

had always wanted, but her parents had only got Sky to make Lucy forget her real home.

"Well, I won't!" Lucy muttered fiercely, gulping back sobs. "They can't make me! Not even with a kitten…"

By now Lucy had cried so much that she was desperately thirsty, and her head ached. She threw on some clothes, and opened her bedroom door quietly. Kieran had gone out to play football, and Mum and Dad were in the garden, looking at the rickety old shed. She could creep down and grab a glass of juice without having to talk to anyone.

Upstairs in her room it had been terribly difficult to tell herself she didn't want a kitten. Downstairs in the kitchen, with Sky staring at her with huge, confused, sad blue eyes, it was completely impossible. Lucy held out for as long as it took to go to the fridge and pour her juice, and drink a few thirsty gulps. But the sight of Sky lost in her too-big basket was irresistible. Lucy put the glass on the table and knelt down beside Sky.

"You don't know what's going on, do you?" she asked gently. "I'm not trying to be mean, honestly," she sighed.

Sky just wanted someone to play with her. She stood up, stretched, and put a paw on Lucy's knee. She gazed at her, her head on one side questioningly. "Maaa?" she mewed pleadingly. Lucy's mum had left a cat toy in the basket, a little jingly ball with ribbons attached to it, and Sky pawed at it hopefully.

Lucy shook her head, smiling. "OK. When it's just you and me, I'll play. But we have to pretend, all right? When Mum and Dad are around, I won't be able to play at all." She looked at Sky. She knew a kitten wouldn't understand that sort of thing, even if she did look very intelligent.

Sky batted at the ball again. Enough talking. She wanted to play.

Lucy danced the ribbons in front of Sky, bouncing the little ball up and down, and sending Sky in crazy, skittering circles all over the kitchen. It was so funny! Lucy hadn't known Nutmeg and Ginger when they were kittens, and she hadn't realized how much more playful a little kitten would be than her two middle-aged, rather plump cat friends. Sky danced, she jumped, she tumbled over and over, attacking the fierce ribbons. "Oh, Sky!" Lucy giggled.

Then she heard voices coming up the garden path. Mum and Dad! Swiftly she stood up, and dropped the jingly ball back into Sky's basket. Sky watched her, puzzled. Was this a new game? Was she supposed to jump into the basket and pull it out again? She dived in, and popped up with a mouthful of ribbons. But Lucy had turned away. She was standing by the table, drinking her juice. Sky waited. Maybe she was supposed to creep up on Lucy, and give her a surprise? Yes! It was a hunting game! She dropped the ball and leaped sneakily out of her basket. Tummy low to the ground and ears pricked with excitement, Sky crept across the kitchen floor – slowly, slowly, now pounce on Lucy's foot!

Just then, Lucy's parents came back into the kitchen. They saw Sky standing on her hind legs, her paws on Lucy's jeans, gazing pleadingly up at her. Lucy was ignoring the kitten entirely, not even looking at her.

Lucy's mum sighed, and went to pick Sky up and stroke her. Sky gave a tiny purr – it was nice to be cuddled – but she was still gazing at Lucy. She was confused. Why didn't Lucy want to play any more? What had gone wrong? It was as though Lucy was a different person. And not a very friendly one.

Chapter Four

By Monday morning, Sky was even more confused. Lucy gave her lots of cuddles and was wonderful to play with when they were on their own, but as soon as anyone else came into the kitchen, she would pretend that she couldn't even see Sky. It was horrible. Sky couldn't help feeling that she must have done something wrong, and she was desperate to make it better. Lucy's mum was trying to keep her in the kitchen until she settled in, but Sky had other ideas. She wanted to follow Lucy everywhere. She trailed determinedly round the house after her, and tried to climb into Lucy's lap every time she sat down.

Lucy was sat at the table eating breakfast, so she tried it again now. But Lucy gave her one quick, unhappy glance and slid her off. Sky crept back to her basket, her whiskers drooping. Kieran made a huffing noise at Lucy, as though he thought she was being stupid. "Here, Sky," he murmured, holding out his hand. "Kitty, kitty."

Sky sniffed his fingers politely, but it

was Lucy she really wanted. She gave him a little purr as he tickled her ears, though. Then she looked up hopefully at Lucy one last time, but she was staring firmly at her cereal bowl.

Lucy's mum was watching them as she buttered some more toast. "We've got to be really careful not to let Sky out of the house today when our new sofa is delivered. She isn't big enough to go outside yet."

Lucy shrugged and saw her mum give her a worried look – she was obviously thinking that Lucy still hadn't changed her mind about Sky. She stared into her cereal, not feeling hungry. Things were going just as she'd planned, and she'd never felt so miserable.

School seemed even worse on Monday. A few times during lessons Lucy glanced at the red-haired girl, hoping she would look back, but she never did. It would be so good to have *someone* to talk to, and the red-haired girl – Lucy was pretty sure she was called Izzy – had seemed friendly before.

At home time Lucy trailed silently down the road after her mum.

"Did you meet anyone nice today?" her mum asked cheerfully.

"No," Lucy sighed. "There *isn't* anyone nice."

"Oh." Her mum looked upset, and Lucy felt a bit guilty.

Lucy glared at the new house as they turned into their road. Then she grinned. Sky was perched on the back of the new sofa in the front room, peering out. Lucy blew her a kiss behind her mum's back as Mum fumbled for her keys, and Sky made a flying leap off the sofa. Eventually, Lucy's mum opened the door, and Sky shot out…

"Oh, catch her, Lucy! We mustn't let her go into the road!"

Lucy tried to grab the kitten, but Sky was too fast for her. Sky danced about all over the garden, enjoying the game of chase. She hadn't had any time with Lucy today, and now Lucy was giving her lots of attention! She hid behind a large plant, her tail swishing excitedly, waiting to jump out.

"Sky! Here puss, puss…" Lucy was creeping closer, hoping to take the kitten by surprise and grab her. She could see Sky's whiskers twitching from behind those big leaves. She jumped behind the plant and her hands closed on nothing as Sky clambered on to the garden wall.

"I'll go and get some cat treats," Lucy's mum said. "Just try to keep her in the garden, Lucy, please!"

"Oh, Sky," Lucy whispered, as Mum disappeared into the house. "I know I haven't been very nice, but don't run off, please. Come on…"

Sky stretched out to sniff Lucy's fingers as Lucy moved slowly closer. Lucy's eyes were bright and wet, and she looked so sad. Sky rubbed her head against Lucy's hand, hoping to cheer her up, and Lucy smiled a little.

"You're just so beautiful," Lucy murmured, as she scooped the kitten gently off the wall and into her arms. She brushed her cheek against Sky's face, and Sky purred happily.

Gazing down the road, Lucy blinked in surprise. There was Izzy! Just turning the corner, with a bigger girl who had the same red hair. They looked so alike that they had to be sisters. Did Izzy live in this road, too? Lucy watched hopefully as the two girls walked along the other side of the road, and stopped at a house a couple of doors down. Izzy suddenly looked round and caught Lucy's eye, and Lucy blushed, embarrassed to be caught staring.

Izzy gave Lucy a quick smile and a tiny wave, almost as though she was shy, too. Then she followed her sister up the path.

Lucy held Sky close, imagining how great it would be to have a friend living just across the road. They could walk to school together. Maybe have sleepovers at each other's houses. She'd always gone by car to her old school, and none of her friends lived anywhere close, not even Ellie. Without thinking, she rubbed Sky gently behind the ears, making her close her eyes and purr with delight.

"So you caught her then?" Lucy's mum was now standing right beside her, holding a packet of cat treats, and smiling.

Lucy looked up, still lost in her thoughts. Then she remembered. Ellie was her friend, not Izzy. She didn't want a kitten to make her forget. She didn't want a kitten at all. She'd told her parents that... She stuffed Sky into Mum's arms, and dashed into the house.

But she could hear Sky mewing, and she longed to rush back and cuddle her again...

Chapter Five

Lucy was staring gloomily at the bean plants in the school garden, and wondering why they bothered growing beans when nobody liked them. Suddenly, somebody tapped her on the shoulder and she jumped.

Izzy grinned at her. "Sorry to scare you. I guess you didn't hear me coming up behind you!"

"Um, no…" Lucy murmured.

"I'm Izzy. Do you live in our road, Hazel Close? I saw you yesterday on the way home from school." Izzy stared eagerly at Lucy.

Lucy nodded. "Yes, we've just moved there," she said quietly.

Izzy didn't seem too bothered by Lucy's flat tone of voice. "That's brilliant. There's no one else my age in our road – well, only Sean Peters and he's worse than no one. It'll be really good to have another girl around."

Lucy smiled. It felt so nice to be wanted!

"So is that gorgeous kitten yours? Is she a Siamese? Have you had her long? You're so lucky, having a kitten!"

Lucy said nothing. She didn't know

what to say. Sky was her kitten, but she wasn't going to be keeping her, was she?

Lucy stared at the ground. There was an uncomfortable silence. Izzy turned to go.

"Orla said you were stuck-up," she said. "I told her you might just be shy, but maybe she was right." She shrugged, and marched off across the garden.

Lucy stared after her, her thoughts racing. Izzy was really nice, and seemed to want to be friends. But now she thought that Lucy was stuck-up. As Izzy opened the garden gate, Lucy dashed after her, trampling most of a row of carrot plants in her rush to catch her up. She caught hold of Izzy's sleeve.

"I'm really sorry, I'm not stuck-up, honestly. I just didn't know what to say." She sighed.

Izzy just looked at her. It wasn't a very encouraging start, but Lucy took a deep breath and began to explain.

"Look, I *really* didn't want to move here. We had to because of my dad's job. I just kept hoping and hoping that my mum and dad were going to change their minds. It's not that I don't think Hazel Close is nice," she added quickly, not wanting to be rude about Izzy's home. "And I guess this is probably a nice school, but I'm really missing my old school, and it's just not the same."

Lucy stopped for breath. Izzy looked curious, so she kept going. "Mum and Dad are trying to persuade me to like it here. They gave me Sky on Saturday, to make me feel better about the move. That's what Mum said." Lucy's eyes filled with tears. "She's supposed to help me forget my old house and my friends and everything."

"Wow," Izzy muttered. "I suppose I'd be miserable if I had to move somewhere totally new."

Lucy nodded.

"But at least you've got Sky. She's gorgeous!" Izzy smiled.

"She is," Lucy agreed. "You're going to think I'm stupid. But – well, I'm pretending I don't like her. That's why I just didn't know what to say when you asked if she was my kitten."

Izzy looked confused. "But why?"

"If Mum and Dad see I really love Sky, they'll think I've stopped missing home and I don't mind staying here," Lucy explained. It *did* sound stupid. She blushed miserably.

"I *guess* that makes sense," Izzy said

rather doubtfully. "So your mum and dad think you don't want her?"

"Whenever they're around I don't play with Sky, or even look at her," Lucy admitted.

Izzy nodded slowly. "But … what's going to happen? If your parents think you don't want her, won't they give her back? You're going to let them?"

"Yes. I mean, I thought I was. I was missing home so much." Lucy sat down on the bench by the gate, and heaved a huge sigh. "Only now I'm not sure I can!"

"Mmmm." Izzy sat down next to her. "I can't imagine giving her back. She's so cute!"

Lucy smiled. "She is, isn't she?" Then she put her chin in her hands and sighed again. "But I can't just change my mind now…"

"You might end up having to stay here, *and* not having a gorgeous kitten," Izzy pointed out.

"I know," Lucy said gloomily.

That night, Lucy waited until her parents were both in the front room, and then crept out of bed. She stole quietly down the stairs, not wanting Kieran to hear her either, and along the hallway to the kitchen.

Sky looked up hopefully as she opened the kitchen door. Lucy had stroked her quickly a few times that evening when no one was looking.

She did wish that Lucy would be nice like that all the time. Sky waited anxiously. Was Lucy going to ignore her again?

Lucy came and sat down next to her basket, and gently stroked the top of Sky's silky head. "Izzy thinks I'm stupid not telling Mum and Dad how much I like you," she told the kitten. "She said she doesn't know how I can pretend. I'm not sure I know either," she added sadly.

Sky climbed out of her basket and clambered up Lucy's leg. She stood on Lucy's lap and butted her chin. That was sure to make her feel better. She licked Lucy, too, just to be certain. There.

Lucy giggled. "Oh, Sky, your tongue's really rough!"

Sky purred as she heard Lucy laughing. It had worked. Lucy was feeling better. She'd seemed so sad before, but now she felt warm and friendly. Sky curled herself into a comfortable ball on Lucy's knee, gave a huge yawn and went to sleep.

Chapter Six

Sky woke up and yawned, stretching her paws lazily. Then she opened her eyes wide, remembering where she was. Lucy's house. The thought of Lucy made her sit up eagerly. Lucy! Where was she? Last night Lucy had cuddled her to sleep on her knee – but now she was back in her basket. Sky hopped out and went to sniff at the kitchen door. She looked up at the handle thoughtfully. Her mum could jump and open door-handles, but Sky wasn't big enough yet. She prowled up and down impatiently. Maybe Lucy would be down soon, and she'd have someone to play with.

When Lucy's mum came downstairs, Sky wove around her feet, nearly tripping her up, but Lucy's mum just laughed. "Are you starving, Sky? Poor kitten! Here you go." She placed a full bowl of kitten food on the floor, and Sky settled down to eat it, keeping one eye on the door.

When Lucy finally came into the kitchen, Sky danced over to her delightedly. *Where were you? I've been waiting for you! Cuddle me!* she mewed.

Lucy gulped. She cast one quick glance at Sky, her tail pointing excitedly straight up, her whiskers twitching with happiness, and then dragged her eyes away. It was so unfair to keep doing this! Sky didn't understand that she could only love her when no one was around. *Quite soon*, Lucy thought sadly, *Sky's going to give up on me...*

Lucy's parents watched as the kitten pawed eagerly at Lucy's leg, and Lucy ignored her again. Lucy's dad gave her mum a serious look and shook his head.

Sky gazed up at Lucy. After last night, she'd been sure that Lucy wouldn't act all strange and cold again. Her tail hung low now as she slunk miserably back to her basket, ignoring the rest of her food.

Lucy didn't touch her breakfast either.

"Wow, you must be starved," Izzy said, watching Lucy munching swiftly through an apple at break.

"Mmmm," Lucy nodded, swallowing. "Didn't eat much for breakfast."

"Well, we've got PE straight after, so you'd better have this as well." She reached into her bag and pulled out a cereal bar.

Lucy gave her a grateful look. "Don't you want it?"

"No. Mum keeps giving me them, but they're yuck. You're welcome," Izzy smiled.

Lucy had looked for Izzy as soon as she got into school that morning, hoping that she would be there already. She'd been delighted when Izzy had seen her and rushed over. When they got into the classroom, Izzy had asked if she wanted to sit next to her – there was room, and she said Mrs Walker wouldn't mind. Orla and Katie looked surprised, but they didn't say anything.

"Hello," Lucy muttered shyly, as she went past. It was the first thing she'd said to them since her first day, and they looked a bit confused.

It was amazing how different school was now she had someone to talk to. Lucy found she actually enjoyed their PE lesson, which was football skills. Izzy was terrible, but she didn't mind and just rolled her eyes at Lucy and giggled hopelessly every time she had to run off across the field after the ball. Lucy was quite good at sporty stuff, and Mr Jackson said he'd have to keep an eye on her for the school team. Lucy couldn't help feeling a bit excited.

When Lucy's mum came to pick her up she was amazed that Lucy came running across the playground to her, rather than trailing slowly out after everyone else. She was with a pretty, red-haired girl who had a massive grin on her face. The red-haired girl grabbed a tall, red-haired woman, who had to be her own mum, then came to join Lucy.

"Did you ask her?" Izzy said anxiously.

Lucy shook her head. "Mum, please can I go to tea with Izzy? She lives across the road from us. Pleeeaase?"

"Oh, Lucy, that sounds great, but maybe another day?" said Mum. "We haven't given Izzy's mum much notice." She smiled apologetically at the red-haired woman.

"Actually, if you don't mind, it's fine by me," Izzy's mum replied. "Izzy mentioned last night that she'd met Lucy, and she'd love to have her over. Lucky it's a Wednesday actually, Izzy's sister Amber has choir so I pick Izzy up.

Usually the girls walk home together. You've just moved in, haven't you?"

Izzy's mum was really friendly, and as the four of them walked home she told Lucy's mum about the neighbours, and which were the nicest shops in the area.

Izzy's mum made a massive tea of pasta, and afterwards Lucy and Izzy hung out in her room. Izzy had a sleepover bed that slid out from underneath hers, and she promised to ask if Lucy could stay the night soon.

"Amber's got a portable DVD player. I bet she'd lend it to us for the night," Izzy told her.

Izzy also had a secret stash of chocolate left over from her birthday, and somehow, munching happily and chatting about the worst teachers at their school, Lucy forgot that she wanted to leave Fairford. It seemed all too soon that Izzy's mum was calling up the stairs to say that Lucy's dad was here to take her home.

"See you tomorrow!" Izzy waved

cheerfully to her as she crossed the road. "Hey, ask your mum if you can walk to school with me and Amber!"

Lucy nodded and waved back. "I will, promise!"

Lucy walked into the kitchen, smiling happily to herself, and then stopped. Mum and Dad both had serious faces. "What is it?" she asked anxiously.

"Lucy, Mum and I have been talking. About Sky." Dad's voice was sad as he looked over at Sky's basket.

Lucy looked, too. Sky was curled-up fast asleep – she was so cute.

"We really hoped that having Sky to play with and look after would make you feel better about the move. We know you're missing Ellie and the others." Her dad sighed. "But I'm sure you'll settle down after a while. Izzy seems very nice – it's great that you're starting to make friends."

Where is Dad going with this? Lucy gazed at her parents.

"Anyway, it looks like we made a mistake with Sky. We should have talked to you about it first, before we went ahead and brought her home."

Lucy blinked stupidly. She could see that Dad was telling her something important, but she couldn't quite seem to understand. Sky was a mistake? Lucy started to feel scared. She looked at Sky, who was still asleep in her basket, although she'd wriggled round and was now lying on her back with her paws in the air. She looked like a toy kitten.

Dad smiled sadly as Sky let out a sleepy half-mew, half-purr. "Luckily the breeder we got Sky from has been very understanding. Tomorrow evening Mum will take Sky back."

Chapter Seven

Lucy felt suddenly cold. It was just like Izzy had said. *You might end up having to stay here, and not having a gorgeous kitten.*

"Oh, Lucy, don't look like that!" Her mum came over and gave her a hug. "We're not cross with you. It was our fault for not talking it over with you first."

No, you don't understand! Lucy wanted to cry out. *Don't give her back! I want to keep her!* But her voice seemed to stick in her throat as her parents went on talking.

Mum stroked Lucy's hair sadly. "Sky deserves a home where she's really wanted. She's such a loving little kitten – she needs someone to give her loads of love back."

Lucy had been about to try to explain, but that made her stop. It was so true. Sky did need a home where she was properly loved. Lucy had a horrible feeling that that special home wasn't here with her. She'd been so mean – Sky didn't know whether Lucy loved her or hated her. *Maybe I just don't deserve to have a kitten,* she thought.

But she had to say goodbye to Sky properly. Even if Sky didn't understand.

Later, Lucy crept downstairs while her parents were in the front room. Sky was in the kitchen, as she usually was at night, and Lucy opened the door quietly.

Sky saw her from her basket, and laid her ears slightly back, and stared up as Lucy came closer in the faint light from the hallway.

Lucy gulped. It was obvious that Sky didn't know what was going on. She crouched down by the basket. "Mum and Dad are right," she whispered to the kitten, running one finger down Sky's back. "You do deserve a better home than this. I've come to say goodbye," she murmured, her eyes filling with tears. One of them dripped on to Sky's nose, making her jump.

"Mrow!" she mewed indignantly, and Lucy laughed and cried at the same time, stifling the strange noise in case her parents heard. Sky's face was so funny, her blue eyes round and cross.

"Ssshh, Sky!" Lucy scooped Sky up, tucking her into her dressing gown. "Come on," she whispered. Lucy looked round quickly as she opened the kitchen door, then scurried up the stairs to her room.

Sky snuggled against Lucy's pyjamas, watching curiously as they went upstairs. She'd never got this far before, the stairs were steep and someone always caught her before she'd struggled up more than a few steps.

Where was she going? Sky purred excitedly as Lucy opened the door to her room and placed her down gently on the floor.

Lucy snuggled under her duvet and watched Sky exploring her bedroom, sniffing her way around the boxes. Having Sky in her room made the little kitten seem much more *hers*, somehow. Lucy could imagine doing her homework up here, with Sky sitting on her windowsill watching the birds, or snoozing on her duvet. Sky clambered on to the bed next to Lucy, and purred lovingly in her ear.

"What am I going to do, Sky?" Lucy murmured sleepily, stroking her. All of a sudden she was so tired. "I wish you could tell me what to do…"

Lucy awoke to find Sky licking her face with her rough little tongue.

"Hey, Sky… That's a nice way to be woken up," she muttered sleepily. "I suppose you want breakfast?" she said, as Sky jumped down off the bed and padded over to the bedroom door.

Lucy threw on her dressing gown, and carried Sky downstairs. When they got to the kitchen she jumped lightly down, and stared demandingly at her food bowl. "Mw-wowl!" she told Lucy firmly.

Lucy grabbed the bag of kitten food from the cupboard. She poured some into Sky's bowl, and fetched herself some juice from the fridge.

Watching Sky busily devouring her breakfast, Lucy wondered if she could bear to let Sky go. She was so lovely! If she told her parents she'd changed her mind, maybe they could keep her...

Her mum came down a few minutes later. "You fed Sky!" she said in surprise. Then she looked at the bag that Lucy had left on the counter. "I suppose I might as well take that to the breeder's with me later. They'll be able to use it up, or give it to her new owner. The basket and things, too, probably," Mum sighed.

Lucy walked quickly out of the kitchen, before she started to cry. Sky's new owner! The person who was going to really love her... Everything was so complicated, Lucy felt she didn't even know what she wanted any more.

The doorbell rang. Izzy and Amber had come to pick her up for school like they'd arranged last night. Sky peeped round the front door, and Izzy nudged Amber. "Look, isn't she gorgeous? Isn't Lucy lucky?"

Amber smiled. "Oh! She's so tiny. You really *are* lucky, Lucy!"

Lucy didn't want to explain what had happened in case she started crying again. "Mmmm!" she said, forcing a smile.

As soon as Amber left them at the school gates to go on to her secondary school, Lucy burst out, "They're taking Sky back!"

"What?" Izzy yelped. "When?"

"Today," Lucy said miserably. "Mum and Dad told me when I got home from your house last night. They said they'd made a mistake, but the people who bred Sky will have her back. Luckily." She sniffed.

Izzy gazed at her in horror. "And you're just going to let them?"

Lucy stared down, noticing that her school skirt had white hairs on it. "I suppose so," she murmured. She was crying *again*!

"You just can't!" Izzy said. "That beautiful kitten, the best present *ever*, and you're letting them take her away!" Izzy's eyes were flashing, and people were staring at them as they walked along the corridor to their classroom.

"You don't understand!" Lucy wailed.

"No, I don't." Izzy dumped her bag on their table.

"Last night I was going to tell them I'd changed my mind about Sky and wanted to keep her," Lucy explained. "I was trying to think how to do it while I was at yours. But when I got home they told me they were going to give Sky back because she needed someone who'd really love her. And they're right! All I've done is make her sad..." she sobbed.

Izzy made a disbelieving noise and put her arm round Lucy. "She didn't look sad the other day when you were cuddling her in your garden! She looked really happy!"

Lucy looked up at her hopefully. "Do you think so?"

Izzy thought for a moment. "Do you think maybe you've been upset about moving house for so long that you're just looking on the wrong side of everything?" she asked.

Lucy felt hurt. It sounded as though Izzy thought she was just being stupid.

"I'm not trying to be mean," Izzy

added hurriedly. "It's just I thought you were actually starting to like being here. You don't *really* hate it, do you?"

Lucy shook her head slowly. "Noooo," she murmured. She looked up at Izzy, feeling confused. She'd been telling herself she hated Fairford for so long, it was hard to admit to someone else that it actually wasn't so bad. "No. Since I made friends with you, it's been fun," she said, smiling. She sat down slowly on the edge of the table, thinking aloud. "And if I could keep Sky, and not have to pretend I didn't like her, it would be even better." Lucy looked shyly up at her friend − Izzy really *was* her friend. "All I have to do is explain to Mum and Dad, and everything will be OK."

Back at Lucy's house, her mum was in the hall searching for her keys, ready to go out shopping. She just had time before Lucy and Kieran came back from school. Mum grabbed her coat from the understairs cupboard. "Where have I put them, puss?" she muttered to Sky. "Oh, there they are, in my pocket all the time!" She sighed, looking at Sky's bright, interested eyes. "I'm going to miss you. But I suppose it's for the best. I'll see you in a while, little one."

Feeling lonely, Sky watched her walk down the road from her perch on the back of the sofa. Then she wandered through the house, looking for something fun to do. She could hear the washing machine rumbling in the kitchen. It would be going round and round! She liked to watch it, so she nudged the door open.

Sky didn't use her basket much during the day – she usually slept on the sofa – so Lucy's mum had tidied it away with her food bowl, and the bag of food. It was all piled up on the counter, ready to take back that evening. Forgetting about the washing machine, Sky looked at the place where her basket was supposed to be, feeling confused. What was going on? Her bowl, her basket, all that food? Didn't they want her any more?

But she liked it here, and she was sure Lucy was beginning to like having her here, too. Determinedly, Sky stalked out of the kitchen. This was her home now, here with Lucy!

Distracted by losing her keys, Lucy's mum hadn't closed the understairs cupboard properly. Sky had never seen this door open before, not even a crack, and she nudged it further open with her nose.

It was full of wellies and bike helmets and coats, and it looked dark and curious. Sky wriggled through the door, and wove herself between the wellies to get further in. At the back was a big wicker basket, full of scarves and hats. Sky climbed into it, and burrowed under Lucy's pink, fluffy hat. Perfect. Now she would stay here until they changed their minds.

Chapter Eight

Lucy and Izzy had agreed to race home after school as fast as they could get Amber to go. As they dashed down their road, Lucy spotted her mum in the driveway, carrying something bulky. It looked awfully like the special box that Sky had come in.

A horrible thought suddenly struck her. What if Mum had taken Sky back earlier than planned? What if Sky had already gone?

She sped ahead of Amber and Izzy, and flung herself through the gates. Her mum had put the box down on the driveway while she closed the garage door, and it was open at the top, its flaps not folded together. It was empty.

Lucy knelt down beside it and looked in, knowing it was no use, but hoping that somehow Sky was there after all, she just wasn't looking properly. But there was no kitten. Lucy was too late. Holding the flaps of the box, Lucy started to cry.

"Lucy!" Her mum was staring at her in horror. "Lucy, what is it? Whatever's the matter?"

Lucy was crying too hard to speak. Izzy and Amber had now caught up with her. Izzy stared down at the box. "Oh no! She's gone already?"

Lucy nodded, her shoulders heaving.

"Girls, what is going on?" Lucy's mum asked.

Izzy looked up at her. "Lucy was going to tell you she didn't want to give Sky back after all. It was all a big mistake."

Lucy's mum gasped. "Lucy? Is this true?" She bent down and pulled Lucy up, putting an arm round her. Lucy clung on to her, still crying quietly.

"Yes," she gulped. "Sorry!"

"But why didn't you say?" her mum asked, confused.

Lucy heaved a shuddering sigh.

"Because I thought you only gave me Sky to make me forget about everyone back home, and I didn't want to forget my friends!"

"That's not why we gave you Sky!" Her mum sounded hurt. "Although … I suppose I can understand how you'd see it like that. Oh, Lucy."

"And now it's too late anyway," Lucy sniffed.

Her mum smiled. "Actually it's not."

Lucy looked up at her in sudden hope. "Can we get Sky back?"

"We don't have to. I was just getting the box out of the garage ready, that's all. Sky's inside somewhere. I'm not sure where, I've only been back ten minutes." Lucy's mum smiled as Lucy, Izzy and Amber dashed over to the front door. "Would you like me to let you in, by any chance?"

The girls burst into the house as soon as she opened the door, calling eagerly for Sky, expecting her to come running. Lucy couldn't help thinking how lovely it was not to have to pretend she didn't care about her lovely kitten. Her kitten! Sky really was hers now!

"Have you found her?" Lucy's mum called a couple of minutes later, once she'd put the box away. "I'd better ring the breeder and tell her we're not bringing Sky back after all."

But Lucy, Izzy and Amber were coming down the stairs, looking worried.

"What's the matter?" Lucy's mum asked, putting her coat away.

"She's not here," Lucy said anxiously. "She couldn't have got out, could she, Mum? She's disappeared. We've looked everywhere."

Her mum shut the cupboard door. "I don't see how she could've got out. She was definitely in when I left, I saw her sitting on the back of the sofa as I went out. Come on, let's look again. She's probably hiding, and playing a game with us."

But they looked and looked, and when Kieran got home he joined in, too, and Lucy's dad a while later. By the time Amber had to drag Izzy home for tea, they still hadn't found her. Sky had disappeared completely.

Tucked away in her warm little nest, Sky had heard everyone searching and calling. She'd almost come out, but maybe they were only trying to find her so they could take her away? The voices calling her name sounded frightened and upset. She thought Lucy was crying, and that made her feel sad, too. Maybe she should come out, and make Lucy feel better? It was so hard to know.

Sky wanted her basket to go back in its proper place in the kitchen. If she waited till they all went to bed, maybe she could go and see if they'd put it back for her? Yes, she would come out then. She was awfully hungry, though, and it was a long time to wait.

Sky tunnelled underneath a

tasselled scarf to make her bed more comfortable. The cupboard was chilly, and so lonely. Oh, she wished Lucy would come and find her – the nice Lucy who stroked her so lovingly, and told her how beautiful she was. That Lucy didn't want to give her away, she was sure!

"Lucy, I know you want to keep looking, but it's really late. You have to go to bed – you've got school in the morning. We'll search outside tomorrow, even though I still don't see how Sky could've got out." Lucy's mum looked anxiously out of the window into the darkness.

Lucy stared out of the window as well, and shivered. It was so dark and cold now. Sky had only been outside the house that once when she'd slipped through the front door. She couldn't stop imagining poor little Sky out there on her own, perhaps hiding under a bush, cold and frightened.

She hugged her mum sadly, then slowly climbed the stairs to her room. Was it only this morning that Sky had woken her up by licking her face? It seemed so long ago. She got into bed, and lay there wishing she hadn't been so stupid. If only she'd told her parents sooner that she'd changed her mind, then maybe this wouldn't have happened.

Sky was determined to wait until everyone had gone to bed before she came out. Then she would go and see if they had put her things back in their proper places. If they hadn't, well, she would go back into the cupboard until they did! But she would find something to eat first.

As the noise in the house died down, she cautiously crawled out of her woolly nest and perched at the edge of the basket, her paws on the rim, listening carefully. Could she sneak out and look around yet? Was it safe? Perhaps she could creep up the stairs and see Lucy, too. She missed her so much!

Sky threaded her way carefully across the cupboard, avoiding a pile of umbrellas, and squeaking with disgust as she bumped into Kieran's muddy football boots. Here was the door – she could see a line of light shining from the hallway.

But shouldn't that line be bigger?

Sky was horrified as she realized that the door to the cupboard was closed. Confused, she scrabbled desperately at the wood, hoping to make the door open again. This door had definitely been open before. Why was it shut now? She yowled in frustration and fury, her tiny claws leaving long scratches in the paint.

Eventually, Sky's howls turned to frightened cries. She was trapped. She couldn't get out. What if she *never* got out?

Lucy! Come and find me! Please! she mewed.

But everyone else in the house was asleep, tired from searching and crying and worrying, and no one heard.

Eventually, Sky clambered back into her safe little nest. She wriggled under Lucy's hat and fell asleep, her paws sore from scratching.

A little later Lucy woke up with a start. She'd been half-dreaming, half-worrying. What if Sky hadn't just slipped out because she spotted an open door? What if she'd run away on purpose?

Lucy knew she had been behaving oddly, playing with Sky one minute, and ignoring her the next. Maybe Sky had given up on her. After all, she had been taken away from her home and her mum, too, and everything had been different and strange, just like it had been for Lucy.

I drove her away, Lucy thought miserably, certain now that this was what had happened. Suddenly she threw back her duvet. "I made her go, and it's up to me to go and find her," she muttered to herself. "I can't leave her out there, thinking I don't love her. This is all my fault."

It was past midnight, and Lucy was pretty sure everyone was asleep. She grabbed her torch, which luckily was on top of one of her boxes, and sneaked down the stairs. She wasn't going to bother getting dressed – her pyjamas were fleecy and warm. She'd just put on her big dressing gown, and her fluffy hat and scarf. She was pretty sure Mum had unpacked them, and they were in that cupboard under the stairs.

Inside the cupboard, Sky was in a restless half-sleep. Then all at once the door opened, and a beam of light cut into the gloom of the cupboard, dazzling Sky for a moment before her eyes adjusted. It was Lucy! Sky was about to run to her, when she remembered the way her basket and food bowl were piled up on the kitchen counter. Did Lucy still want her? She peered out from under Lucy's hat, her eyes big and round and hopeful in the dark.

"It's my fault," Lucy whispered to herself. "Poor Sky. All because I was so stubborn."

Sky heard her name, and Lucy's sad voice. But what did it mean?

Lucy spotted the basket, and flashed the torch over the top, looking for her hat and scarf. It was cold outside and she might be out searching for a while – she wasn't coming back until she'd found Sky and brought her home!

Then she stopped with a gasp. Peering out from under her hat was a tiny creamy-white head. Big blue eyes blinked at her uncertainly.

"Sky!" Lucy breathed. "There you are! Mum was right, you didn't get out after all! Oh, Sky, we've been looking for you all night." She crouched down next to the basket, and looked closely at her. "Are you all right? Were you stuck in here? Why didn't you call?"

Sky watched Lucy warily. Her voice sounded loving, but a little sad as well. *Please don't give me back...* she mewed. *I want to stay!*

"Were you hiding?" Lucy asked slowly. "Because you didn't know what was going on? Oh, Sky, I'm so sorry..." She reached out one finger, very gently, and rubbed Sky under her chin. "It's all going to be fine now, I promise. No more pretending I don't love you, because I really, really do. I know I do. Please come out!"

Sky stood up unsteadily on the pile of hats and gloves, and mewed again. *I'm so hungry!* she told Lucy.

"You must be starved," Lucy muttered. Very gently, she picked Sky up, cradling her close.

Sky could feel Lucy's heart beating as she carried her to the kitchen. Her own heart was thumping anxiously, too. Where would her basket be? She sat tensely in Lucy's arms as she opened the door, and turned on the kitchen light. Then she howled in dismay. It was piled up on the counter still, with her bowl and food bag. They were still going to give her away!

"Hey, hey, Sky, what's wrong?" Lucy asked. "Oh! Your basket. Does it look strange up on the counter like that? It's all right, look." Whispering soothingly and cuddling the tiny kitten in one arm, Lucy took Sky's toys out of the basket and put it back in its warm corner by the radiator. Sky stopped crying, and leaned over Lucy's arm to sniff it suspiciously. It seemed right. Good. Now all Lucy had to do was get her food bowl.

"Lucy!" Lucy's mum was at the kitchen door, her dressing gown half-tied, looking worried. "What are you doing?" she said. "Oh, you've found her! Where was she?" She turned to Lucy's dad, who had followed her downstairs. "Lucy's found Sky!"

Lucy carried her kitten over for her mum to stroke. "She was in the cupboard under the stairs. She must have been there all that time!" She looked seriously at her parents. "I think she was hiding because she didn't know whether we wanted her or not," she said quietly. "But we really do, don't we?"

"Of course we do," said Mum.

Her dad poured some food into Sky's bowl. "I bet she's starving."

Sky started to eat, gulping down the food, then looking hopefully for more.

"It's not that long till breakfast, Sky, don't worry!" Lucy giggled. She looked up at her mum and dad. "Can Sky sleep on my bed?" she begged.

Her mum nodded. "If you get back to bed right this minute! In fact, I think we should *all* get back to bed!"

Sky rubbed her head against Lucy's chin as she carried her upstairs. She could tell how happy Lucy was.

As Lucy snuggled up under her warm duvet, Sky curled up next to her on the pillow and purred loudly. There was no place either of them would rather be! Lucy and Sky were home.

Ginger the Stray Kitten

For Sophie

Chapter One

"Are we going past the farm today?" Rosie asked her gran hopefully. They had a few different ways back from school to Gran's house, but the lane past the farm was Rosie's favourite. That was the good thing about Gran picking her up from school while Mum was at work. Gran wasn't usually in a rush, and she didn't mind walking slowly while Rosie stopped to look at any cats she happened to meet on the way. Rosie loved cats and was desperate for one of her own, but she hadn't managed to persuade her mum yet.

Gran smiled at her. "Oh, I suppose we could go home that way. I could do with picking up some eggs from Mrs Bowen. I might make a cake tonight, as it's the weekend." She looked down at Rosie, and said thoughtfully, "But you know how she likes to chat, Rosie. Are you sure you won't get bored?"

Rosie looked up at her in surprise, and realized that Gran was teasing. Gran knew that Rosie loved going to the farm, because while she was talking to Mrs Bowen, Rosie could go and watch the stray cats in the farmyard.

There were lots of them, and Gran said they were called feral cats because they weren't anyone's pets. Rosie had never managed to count them all, as they were so hard to see, but she thought there were probably about twenty of them. Mrs Bowen put food out occasionally, but mostly they lived on the mice they caught in the barns.

Rosie loved to imagine that the cats belonged to her, but they weren't really very friendly. If she sat on the foot step of the old rusty tractor for ages and ages, they might prowl past her, but none of them would come to be stroked.

One of the prettiest cats, a tabby with beautiful spotty markings, had given birth to a litter of kittens about five weeks before. Rosie had heard them mewing in the barn, but she hadn't been able to see them for ages, as the tabby cat had hidden them under some old hay bales that were stored in there.

Now the kittens were all dashing about the farmyard, and they weren't quite as shy as the older cats. Rosie was really hoping that she could tame one of them. She couldn't help dreaming of taking a kitten home for her own pet.

She knew which one she wanted most of all – the gorgeous little ginger boy kitten. He was so sweet – he had gingery-creamy fur with darker ginger stripes, and an amazingly bright pink nose. His eyes were very green and very big, and Rosie thought he was the most handsome cat she'd ever seen.

Sometimes people called Rosie Ginger because of her long, curly red hair. Mum had always told her that her red hair was lovely and different, and that she'd like it when she was older, but Rosie wasn't so sure. Then she had seen the kitten. She felt like she and the kitten were a pair, with their ginger colouring. They were ginger and proud of it!

She wished the ginger kitten would let her stroke him. She could just imagine how soft his fur would be. The other day he'd actually come close enough to sniff at her fingers, but he'd darted off again without letting Rosie touch him.

Gran called hello at Mrs Bowen's back door, which was half open, and Rosie looked eagerly around the farmyard. She had something special for the cats today, and she was really hoping she could tempt the ginger kitten to come over to her. Rosie had noticed at lunch that her friend Millie had ham sandwiches. Mum usually put jam sandwiches in Rosie's lunch box, because they were her favourite, but she couldn't help thinking that the kitten would love Millie's sandwiches, the ham smelled really nice. Millie was picking at the ham with a bored expression.

"Don't you like your sandwiches?" Rosie asked, a plan starting to form in the back of her mind.

"I wanted peanut butter, but my brother had nicked it all," Millie sighed. "I hate ham…"

"Do you want to swap? I've only got one left, but it's jam," Rosie offered hopefully.

"You sure?" Millie looked delighted. "I didn't know you liked ham. You can have both of them!"

Rosie had slowly eaten one of the sandwiches, and then tucked the other one away in her lunch box.

"Didn't you like it after all?" Millie asked.

Rosie leaned over closer to her. The kitten felt like a special secret, and she didn't want everyone to know. "I'm saving it. Remember the gorgeous ginger kitten I was telling you about that lives on the farm on the way back to my gran's house? He came right up to me the other day, and I bet if I had some food he might even let me stroke him. You don't mind, do you?"

Millie shook her head. "Of course not! Oh, you're so lucky, going to see kittens. Are they tiny?"

"The lady who owns the farm thinks they're about five weeks old. They're so cute! Maybe your mum would let you come home with us and see them

136

one day? I'm sure Gran wouldn't mind. She could do tea for you as well."

Now Rosie carefully unwrapped Millie's sandwich, and started to crumble it into little bits, very gently, trying to keep as still and quiet as she could. It didn't take long for the cats to get a whiff of the delicious, meaty smell.

Rosie caught a movement out of the corner of her eye, just a streak of black fur. It was one of the kittens, popping its head round the tractor wheel, trying to see what that yummy smell was. Suddenly, several more little cat faces popped up, their whiskers twitching as they sniffed the air.

Rosie threw a bit of sandwich on the ground a little way away, and the closest kitten, the black one, pounced and swallowed it whole. Then he looked up for more. All the other kittens padded a few steps forward, not wanting to miss out. This time Rosie dropped the food closer, and one of the tabby kittens darted in and grabbed it, running back to a safe distance before she dared to stop and eat.

Rosie's heart thumped with delight as she saw her favourite ginger kitten patter across the farmyard, eager to join in. She tried to throw the next piece close to him, but the tabby kitten got there first and gobbled it up, right under his nose. The ginger kitten gave Rosie a piteous stare. *I'm so hungry*, he seemed to be saying. *Pllleeeease feed me...*

This time Rosie threw him an extra-large piece. The ginger kitten held it down with one paw, and hissed protectively when the others circled round him. Rosie laughed out loud – his furious little face was so funny – and the kittens looked up at her in shock, their eyes wide. Then they all shot off back into their hiding places.

"Oh no!" Rosie muttered to herself, wishing she hadn't been so noisy.

But the ginger kitten had only run a couple of steps away from his piece of sandwich, and now he eyed it uncertainly. Food – but also noisy girl. What was he supposed to do? He eyed her thoughtfully. He'd seen her before, she came quite often. She didn't usually make a noise, and she was quiet now.

She wasn't even moving. And she still had lots more of that sandwich.

He darted over and gulped down the rest of his piece, then looked around. His brother and sisters were hiding still. If he went a bit closer, while they weren't here, he might get *more* sandwich… Nervously, ready to run in case she made that loud noise again, he edged closer, his eyes on the ham.

Rosie carefully tossed him a little bit, much nearer to her feet this time.

The kitten stared at her suspiciously. Rosie looked back. Maybe it was too close. But then the kitten moved one paw forward cautiously, and then the other, and then he was just close enough. He started to gobble the sandwich, with one eye on Rosie all the time.

When it was all gone he sat up and eyed her hopefully, licking his whiskers. He cast a quick look behind him. The others were all watching, but they weren't coming any closer. The food was all his! He knew it was risky, but the sandwich was too delicious. He had to have more!

Rosie couldn't help smiling. He was only about a metre away from her foot, almost close enough to touch. This time, instead of throwing the sandwich, she just held out her hand with the last few pieces in.

The ginger kitten stared at her nervously. What was he supposed to do now? The smell of that sandwich was so good. He could just run up and grab it, couldn't he? He skittered forward, his whiskers trembling, and quickly licked up a few crumbs from Rosie's hand, before stepping back to watch her again.

Then he heard a noise and looked round. His brother and sisters were starting to creep closer! They'd seen that he wasn't afraid, so they were getting braver, too. If he didn't wolf that sandwich down fast, he might have to share it.

The ginger kitten hurried back to Rosie and started to eat as fast as he could, licking the crumbs away with his rough little tongue. Rosie had to try hard not to giggle – he was tickling her!

In a few seconds the kitten had eaten the lot. He glared at her hand, obviously wondering when it was going to produce some more.

"Sorry, it's all gone," Rosie whispered. "But I'll bring you some more next time. I bet Mum would let me have ham sandwiches if I asked, and I'd give them all to you."

The kitten eyed her expectantly, and Rosie stretched out her hand. He licked it, but there was no more ham.

Rosie gently stroked the top of his head, and he jumped in surprise, looking up at her with enormous emerald eyes. *What was that for?* he seemed to be saying. Rosie guessed he just wasn't used to being stroked. He didn't know that she was trying to be nice. It made Rosie feel sad.

"Rosie! Where are you?" It was Gran, calling from the farmhouse door. The ginger kitten raced for the safety of the barn at top speed, chasing after his brother and sisters, and Rosie sighed as she got up. Still, she had managed to stroke him! That was a first. He was so little and thin, but his fur had been gorgeously soft, exactly as she'd imagined. More than ever, Rosie wished she could have a kitten just like him…

Chapter Two

Rosie thought about the ginger kitten all weekend. It was such a big step that he'd let her stroke him! Maybe she really would be able to tame him. He was very young, after all.

She sat dreamily at the kitchen table, while Mum was writing a shopping list, drawing pictures of the kitten.

It was so hard to get his stripes right,
she had to keep starting again.

"That's beautiful, Rosie!" Mum said,
leaning over.

Rosie shook her head. "His face
ought to be more of a peachy colour.
I don't have the right pen for it."

"Is it a real cat then?" Mum asked.
"One of the ones you
see on the way
home from
school?"

"He's a kitten at Mrs Bowen's farm," Rosie explained. "You know, the little farm down the lane, about two minutes' walk from Gran's house? There's five of them altogether. You'd love them, Mum."

She looked hopefully at her mother. Maybe if Mum came and saw how cute the kittens were, she'd let them take the little ginger one home. If only Rosie could tame him...

"He does look cute," her mum agreed. "Just be careful though, won't you? Those wild cats have probably got all sorts of horrible bugs."

Rosie sighed. That didn't sound particularly hopeful...

Rosie's mum couldn't understand why she was so keen to get to school on Monday morning.

"I'm going to be at work early, at this rate," she said. "What's got into you, Rosie? Usually it's me telling you to get a move on, not the other way around."

Rosie just smiled. The sooner she was at school, the sooner it would be home time and she could persuade Gran to take her to the farm again. Or it felt that way anyway, even though she knew that really it didn't make any difference how early she got there.

She'd made sure Mum bought ham for her sandwiches this week, and she'd begged for an extra yoghurt so she could save both sandwiches and not have her tummy rumbling all afternoon.

Luckily, Gran didn't mind going to the farm again, and chatting with Mrs Bowen. Rosie ran ahead as they went down the lane that led past the farm, calling to her gran to hurry.

"I can't walk any faster, Rosie," said Gran. "You really do love those cats, don't you?" She was frowning a little as she said it, but Rosie was thinking about whether the ginger kitten would remember her and didn't notice.

It seemed to Rosie that the cats appeared more quickly this time when she sat down on the old tractor. Obviously they remembered her as the food person. The ginger kitten was the first to appear, his wide, white whiskers twitching with anticipation. Rosie wished he wasn't so nervous of her, and that she could take him home and look after him. She crumbled the sandwich and scattered a few pieces around, hoping that again he'd be brave enough to come really close.

The kitten sniffed the air delightedly. More ham! And the others weren't as brave as he was, so he could have most of it to himself. He was sure the girl wasn't dangerous – she *had* touched him last time, but very gently. It had been quite nice. He'd even let her stroke him again, if there was ham.

Rosie watched hopefully as he crept forward, and she held out a particularly yummy-looking piece of ham. The kitten nibbled it delicately, then bumped her hand with his forehead, as if to say thank you. Rosie held out her left hand with some more sandwich, and carefully rubbed behind his ears with the other.

The kitten looked up at her, still confused about why she wanted to stroke him like this, but not minding too much. He even purred, just a little. He was a bit itchy behind the ears, and she was rubbing exactly the right spot.

He finished the last of the sandwich and stared at Rosie, sniffing her fingers to see if more food would appear. When it didn't, he yawned, showing a very pink tongue, and jumped on his little tabby sister's tail, starting a kitten wrestling match.

Rosie watched them, giggling quietly to herself. They were so funny! Maybe tomorrow she would bring a piece of string for them to chase, she was sure they would like that.

The kittens suddenly scattered, and Rosie turned to see her gran coming out of the farmhouse and waving goodbye to Mrs Bowen. Gran looked a bit worried, and Rosie jumped up.

"What's the matter?" she asked, as they headed for the gate into the lane.

Gran looked down at her, and sighed. "I've been meaning to talk to you about this for a while, Rosie," she said. "Mrs Bowen is moving – she's going to live with her son in the village. The farmhouse is a bit too big for her now she's on her own."

Rosie stared up at Gran in surprise. She couldn't imagine the farm without Mrs Bowen. "Oh... So who's going to live at the farm now?" she asked. "Is Mrs Bowen selling it?" Rosie looked back at the farm gate. There was no For Sale sign up.

"No..." Gran hesitated. "Well, yes, I suppose she is. The land has been sold to a developer – they're going to knock down the farm buildings and put up some houses instead. Mrs Bowen signed the contract with them a little while ago, and she's been gradually packing her things up and moving them over to her son's house. She's leaving the farm this week."

Rosie gasped. It was all happening so quickly. Then a horrible thought struck her. "But Gran, what's going to happen to the cats? They won't stay around when the farm's a building site! Where will they go?"

"It's all right, Rosie," Gran said soothingly, putting an arm round her shoulders. "Mrs Bowen's asked the people from the Animal Rescue Centre in Wilmerton to rehome the cats. They're going to come and collect them tomorrow, she told me. It'll be much better for the cats, you know. They'll check them over, and find proper homes for the kittens. As for the older cats, they'll try and find someone with farm buildings or stables who'll have them as outdoor cats, like they are here."

Rosie nodded. "But I won't see them any more," she said sadly, her voice quivering. "Not even the little ginger kitten, and he was starting to like me, Gran, he really was. I … I even thought of trying to take him home, if I could persuade Mum…"

"I'm not surprised he liked you, considering you were feeding him all your sandwiches." Gran smiled at her. "Mrs Bowen does have windows and I'm not blind, Rosie!"

"Oh." Rosie looked up at Gran, her cheeks a little pink. "You won't tell Mum, will you?" she asked.

"Well, no. But I think you'd have been better off eating the sandwiches yourself and buying some cat treats with your pocket money," Gran suggested.

"I shouldn't think your mother would like to know she was making sandwiches for a tribe of wild cats."

"It won't matter now anyway," Rosie said tearfully. "I'll never see any of them again!"

When Mum picked Rosie up from Gran's that night, she was surprised by the quiet, sad little figure who trailed down the stairs.

"What's up, Rosie? Did you have a bad day at school?" she asked.

Rosie shook her head.

"You go and get your things, Rosie," Gran suggested, and by the time Rosie had packed up her homework and her pencil case, Gran had obviously told Mum what was going on, because she didn't ask again.

Rosie stared miserably out of the car window as they drove back to their house, which was a bit further out of the village than Gran's. The rescue centre people would be thinking about new homes for the kittens already, she supposed. All those lucky people, who'd be getting gorgeous kittens. Rosie wondered who would get to adopt the ginger kitten. Maybe there'd be a girl her age. But she was sure no one would ever love him as much as she did. She was so jealous.

Suddenly, Rosie sat up straight, staring out of the front window in excitement. Why shouldn't that girl be her? The kitten needed a new home, and he already liked her. She could name him Ginger! It was perfect!

Except that she would have to persuade her mum, of course.

"What is it, Rosie?" her mum asked. "A rabbit didn't run in front of the car, did it? I didn't feel anything."

"What? No! Mum, can we have a kitten?" Rosie gabbled. "Please? All Mrs Bowen's cats need new homes, and we'd be a perfect new home, wouldn't we?"

Mum didn't say anything for a minute, and Rosie stared at her hopefully. At least she hadn't said no at once.

"I don't know, Rosie," Mum murmured at last. "It would be nice to have a pet – but those kittens are wild.

They aren't used to people. I don't know if we'd be the right home. Someone who knows more about cats would be better, I think."

"We could learn about cats!" Rosie pointed out eagerly. "And those kittens really, really need homes, Mum. Did Gran tell you the rescue centre people are coming to get the cats tomorrow? They'll hate being in a rescue centre, in cages. There's one of the kittens, Mum, he's really sweet, and he's already almost tame. He lets me stroke him and he even eats out of my hand. He'd be a brilliant pet!"

"Well, I'll think about it. Maybe we could go and see them, see how tame they really are. I'm not sure I want a wild kitten climbing my curtains…"

Rosie beamed. She was sure that Ginger was hers already. He was so cute Mum just wouldn't be able to resist him!

Back at the farm, the ginger kitten curled up next to his mother and brother and sisters, in a pile of hay in the old barn. It made a cosy nest, and he licked his paw sleepily. He was thinking about that girl, and wondering if she would come back tomorrow. She might bring more food, and maybe she would stroke his fur again. It was nice when she did that, a bit like his mother licking his ears.

He snuggled up closer to his tabby sisters, and closed his eyes. The hay was soft and warm, and he quickly fell asleep, never dreaming that everything was about to change.

Chapter Three

The next morning, the kittens were startled awake by the noise of a vehicle driving into the yard. Mrs Bowen didn't have a car, and she took most of her eggs to the village shop to sell, so very few people drove up to the farm. The kittens blinked at each other, then peered blearily over the edge of their straw nest. The kittens' mother, the spotted tabby cat, went to stick her nose round the old barn door. The ginger kitten pattered after her, eager to see what was going on. He wriggled between his mother's front paws, staring out into the yard.

Mrs Bowen was standing by the back of a van, next to two girls. One of the girls opened up the doors and started to unload some odd-looking boxes. The van smelled strange, the kitten thought. He'd never smelled anything quite like it before. And what were those wire box things?

His mother was tense beside him, her whiskers pricked out as she watched what was going on. His brother and sisters were starting to mew and cry back in their nest, as they smelled the fear scents on their mother and the other older cats who were watching, too. They just didn't trust humans. The tabby cat backed into the barn so that her ginger baby wasn't between her paws any more, and butted him hard with her nose.

He looked round in surprise. What was the matter? Why was she pushing him? Was it a game? Then he saw that her eyes were wide with fear, and the fur had risen all along her back. This was no game. She swiped the kitten with her paw, sending him sliding out into the yard, and then she hissed at him with her ears laid flat back against her head. It was quite clear what she was telling him to do.

Run!

The ginger kitten scooted quickly out of the barn door, heading for the old tractor. The tyre had come away from the wheel, and the ginger kitten had found this wonderful hiding place while he was playing at jumping out on top of his sisters. There he waited, his heart thudding with fear, trying to work out what was going on.

His mother had darted back into the barn to try and fetch his brother and sisters, and some of the other cats were trying to make a run for it, too. But as soon as they'd seen that the cats knew they were there, the two girls had quickly put a net round the barn door. Now they'd put on big gloves, and they were catching the cats with strange things that gripped them round the neck.

Ginger watched in horror as one by one his brother and sisters were caught, and placed into wire cages. He could hear them mewing frantically as the cages were loaded into the van. Then one of the girls walked right up to the tractor where he was hiding.

The kitten edged back as far as he could go, trembling. He didn't want the girl to see him, but now *he* couldn't see what was happening. Where were they taking his brother and sisters? Were they all in that horrible-smelling van? Had they caught his mother, too? He couldn't see! His tail thrashed from side to side as the girl walked past, searching – for him, maybe. Ginger curled himself into the tiniest ball, his eyes wide with fear.

"I've just caught the last one. I'm glad I had my gloves, she was struggling like anything!" shouted a voice from across the farmyard. Ginger then listened as the girl walked away from the tractor and the van doors slammed shut.

As the van drove off, a small bright-pink nose peeped out from the wheel of the tractor. Ginger watched the van rattling out of the farm gate, carrying his brother and sisters away from him, and gave a miserable little mew. Should he try to follow them? But he was sure his mother hadn't been happy about where they were going. Where was his mother? Maybe she'd managed to find a hiding place, too? Perhaps she would come and get him now the people had gone? Or should he try to find her?

Ginger crept out of his hiding place, and started to search the farmyard. It smelled empty, and there was no sign of any other cats at all. But he couldn't believe that his mother had left him. She wouldn't! Even if they had caught her, she would have got away somehow.

He wandered round the outside of the barn, mewing sadly, and wishing she would come back soon, because he was getting hungry. Maybe she'd gone hunting for a nice mouse for his breakfast. Yes, that was probably it.

As the morning wore on, he got hungrier and hungrier. He searched around for his mother and mewed pitifully for her, but still she didn't come.

At last he went a little closer to the farmhouse, drawn by the smell from the bins. Mrs Bowen had been clearing out her fridge and cupboards, and there were some black plastic bags lying there. The kitten pawed at one of them hopefully and clawed a little hole, hooking out some old cheese. He nibbled at it. It wasn't very nice, but it was better than nothing.

He ate all of it, his whiskers twitching at the strange taste. He wished the girl would come back and feed him some more of that delicious ham. He had been surprised when she stroked him, but he'd quite liked it. If she came back now, he wouldn't be all on his own and she might stroke him some more. Oh, if only *somebody* would come!

Rosie practically towed Gran to the farmyard after school.

"All right, Rosie, all right! But we can't stay long. Mrs Bowen is still busy packing. She's moving tomorrow. She won't want us bothering her today," Gran said firmly.

"I know, but I must just find out about the kittens, whether the people did come today. Mum said we might be able to pop into the rescue centre on the way home!" Rosie looked up at her gran with shining eyes. "If she likes him, we could even take him home this afternoon!"

Gran smiled. It was lovely to see Rosie so excited, although she wasn't sure Rosie's mum would agree to a kitten straight away.

Mrs Bowen waved to them from the kitchen window. She was piling china carefully into a big box, and looked a bit hot and bothered.

"Did they come?" Rosie asked her excitedly. "Did they take all the kittens to the rescue centre?"

Mrs Bowen smiled. "Oh yes, dear. This morning."

"Have you got the address?" Rosie asked hopefully. "Mum says we can go and look at the kittens – she might even let me keep one of them! The sweet little ginger one, you know?"

Mrs Bowen wrote it down, and Rosie folded up the piece of paper and tucked it carefully in her pocket.

Mum had said she'd try and leave work a bit early so they could go to the rescue centre that evening, and now Rosie sat by Gran's front window, watching for her car. When her mum arrived at last, she dashed out to meet her.

"The kittens are at the rescue centre! I've got the address, Mum. Come on, they're only open until six!" she cried.

Her mum laughed. "All right! But remember, Rosie, we're just looking. I know you hope we'll be taking that kitten home, but I still need to think about this. And anyway, I can't imagine we'll be allowed to take one of them yet. They'll need to be checked by a vet, to make sure they're fit and healthy."

Rosie nodded. "But at least let's go and see!" she pleaded.

Secretly she was sure that as soon as her mum saw Ginger, she would give in. Maybe they wouldn't be able to take him home today, but they could still tell the rescue centre people that they wanted him!

The rescue centre was in the next village. The girl at the reception desk knew about the kittens, and she smiled at Rosie's eager questions.

"I'm sure you can go and see them," she said. "We wouldn't usually let people visit the kittens until we'd checked them over, but seeing as you already know them..." She led Rosie and her mum through to a room at the back, with large cat-runs in it.

Rosie spotted the tabby mother cat at once. She was prowling up and down the run, looking anxious.

"Oh, she really doesn't like being shut in. And she must be upset that she's not with her kittens," Rosie said sadly.

The girl from the rescue centre nodded. "I know. But because she's a feral cat we need to separate her kittens from her now, before they get too old. It's so the kittens can get used to humans and to give them the best chance of settling in when they go to their new homes. They're in that run at the end, want to see them?"

"Oh, yes... Come and see, Mum!" Rosie whispered, grabbing her mum's hand and pulling her along.

"Oh, they are sweet!" her mum agreed, peering through the wire. "Look at that little black one!"

But Rosie was staring anxiously into the run. There were four kittens in the basket, curled up asleep – one black, and three tabbies. There was no lovely little ginger kitten.

Ginger wasn't there!

Chapter Four

"Don't cry, Rosie," Mum said gently as they walked back to the car.

Rosie was trying not to cry, but there were just a few tears that she couldn't seem to stop. She was thinking about what could've happened at the farm when the cats were caught.

Why hadn't Ginger been with them? Probably he'd found a sneaky way out of the barn and slipped away. But why? Perhaps he'd just been frightened of the rescue centre people, but it was also possible that he had stayed behind at the farm to wait for her. Maybe he hadn't wanted to go with the other cats because of her, because she'd been feeding him and playing with him.

She had read about feral cats on the internet and knew that they were good hunters, but Ginger was too young to hunt properly for himself. His mother would still have been catching food for her kittens, and showing them how to chase the mice in the barns. Without her to feed him, he might starve. Rosie nodded firmly to herself. She had to go back to the farm. She just had to find him, however long it took.

Rosie was determined to stop and look for the kitten the next day, but she and Gran got a shock when they reached the farm. Gran had come another way to collect Rosie from school, because she needed to go to the shops, and they both stopped in surprise as they came close.

"Goodness, that's gone up quickly!" Gran exclaimed.

A huge wire fence was now surrounding the farmyard, covered in big notices about wearing hard hats, and no children playing on the building site. It was a building site already!

Rosie pressed her face up against the wire fence. The farmyard was deserted, with no sign of life at all.

"Can't we go in and look for him?" she asked Gran.

"No, Rosie, look – it says no one can go in." Gran sighed. "We'll just have to keep coming by and hope we spot him – or perhaps we could ask the builders to keep an eye out. There's no one here now, but I'm sure there will be soon, otherwise they wouldn't have bothered to put the fence up, would they?"

Gran was right. The next day, a couple of men in yellow hard hats were wandering round the building site with a little machine that beeped, which Rosie and Gran guessed was some sort of clever measuring gadget. It took them ages to catch the men's attention, but at last one of them came over.

"Yes?" he asked.

"Have you seen a kitten?" Rosie said nervously. "There were some cats here, and they were taken to a rescue centre, but we think one of the kittens ran away and..." She trailed off. "We just wondered if you'd seen him? A ginger kitten?"

"No, sorry." The builder turned away. Rosie didn't dare call him back, even though she wanted to.

"Could you keep an eye out for him, please!" Gran called, and Rosie squeezed her hand gratefully. She'd wanted to ask that, too.

They carried on walking, Rosie looking back sadly every so often. They seemed to be able to see that fence for ages.

"Don't give up hope, Rosie," Gran told her. "You never know."

But Rosie couldn't help feeling that her chances of finding Ginger were getting smaller and smaller. What if he had escaped before the fence went up. Maybe he wasn't there at all!

Ginger was hiding between two hay bales in the barn, peering out occasionally, and trembling as the men's heavy boots thumped past the door. Who were they? And why were they stamping and crashing round his home? He wished his mother and his brother and sisters would come back, but he was almost sure now that they were gone for ever. If his mother had still been here, she would have come to find him by now, wouldn't she?

He had hidden in the barn when the men came to put the fence up, and he'd dashed back there again this morning when they returned. He didn't dare do more than poke his nose out occasionally to see if they'd gone. He was starving, and it was getting harder to find anything to eat in the bin bags by the farmhouse.

There were voices outside now. Were more people coming? He shivered. He wanted the farm to go back to being quiet and safe like it was before. He listened miserably, but then his ears pricked up. He knew that voice. It was the girl! She was there! Maybe she'd known he was hungry and had brought him some more sandwiches? He edged nervously round the barn door, the fur on his back ruffling up.

The men were still there, and the girl was talking to one of them. If only they would go, he could run over to her. Perhaps she didn't know he was here. He mewed a tiny mew, hoping she would hear. But he didn't dare call more loudly in case the men saw him.

No! The girl was turning away. She was going!

Rosie walked sadly away down the lane with Gran, leaving the kitten staring desperately after her.

The girl had gone, and Ginger didn't know if she would come back. He felt so small and scared, and very, very alone...

Chapter Five

On Friday Gran was waiting outside school for Rosie as usual. It was spitting with rain, and Rosie was taking a while. She and Millie were among the last few to come out, and Millie had her arm round her friend.

"Rosie's really upset about Ginger," she explained to Rosie's gran.

"I just don't think I'm ever going to see him again," Rosie whispered sadly.

"You mustn't give up!" Millie said firmly.

Millie's mum had come up and was giving Rosie a concerned look. "Is everything OK, Millie?" she asked, and Millie explained about Ginger being missing.

"Poor little thing," her mum murmured. "Have you tried putting food out to tempt him, just in case he's still around?"

Rosie lifted her head. "No! No, we haven't, we should try that! Can we do that today, Gran? Oh no, I should have saved my sandwiches for him!"

"You could buy some cat treats in the pet shop!" Millie suggested.

"Sammy loves those, especially the salmon-flavour ones."

"Please!" Rosie begged. "I'll pay you back out of my pocket money, Gran."

Gran smiled. "I think I can afford some cat treats. Come on then."

"Oh, I wish I could come with you, but I've got dancing," Millie said. "I'd love to see him. I bet he'll come out for those cat treats."

"Thanks for the brilliant idea," Rosie told her gratefully, and she and Gran set off to the pet shop.

"Call me and let me know if you see him!" Millie yelled after them, and Rosie turned back to wave. Millie had understood at once why she was so upset. She adored her fluffy, white cat, Sammy. He'd been lost for a couple of days last year, and it had been awful.

Rosie chose the salmon treats, like Millie had suggested. Sammy was gorgeous and podgy and liked his food – Ginger was sure to like them, too. Then they walked quickly over to the farm. From a long way down the lane, they could hear banging and the rumbling sounds of big vehicles. Rosie and Gran exchanged a look and speeded up to see what was going on.

The farm looked so different. The builders were knocking down the barn! A huge, yellow digger was thundering past them on the other side of the fence – even Rosie felt scared by how big and loud it was. How would a kitten feel!

"Oh no!" Rosie cried. "That's where the cats all used to sleep." She watched as the digger tore at the walls. She clung on to the wire fence, pressing her face against it so hard she could feel the wires marking her forehead, and looked frantically around the building site. She still couldn't see the kitten.

"He's not there, is he?" she asked, her voice shaking. "You don't think he was in the barn, when they – when they started pulling it down…"

Gran stared through the fence at the builders and their machines, and sighed. "I don't know, Rosie. He could just be hidden away somewhere because he's frightened. It's so noisy, he might want to come out, but he doesn't dare." She put her arm round Rosie.

"Try the cat treats," she suggested gently. "Why don't you scatter a few through the fence? Maybe the smell will tempt him." She helped Rosie tear open the tough packet. "Goodness, I should think he'd smell that from miles away, they're very fishy, aren't they?"

The treats did smell very strong, and Rosie pushed a few through the mesh of the fence. Then they waited, watching the builders in their bright yellow vests and hard hats as they cleared away the broken pieces of wood that were all that was left of the kitten's home. But there was no sign of Ginger – no long, white whiskers peeping out from behind a hay bale, no ginger tail flicking round the corner of the farmhouse. He was nowhere to be seen. After ten minutes of waiting and calling, Gran turned to Rosie.

"It's starting to rain harder, Rosie. We'd better go, but we'll try again. Maybe your mum will bring you over tomorrow or on Sunday. We won't give up."

Rosie nodded, feeling slightly better. She would never give up on Ginger.

Even though he was only across the farmyard, Ginger hadn't seen them. He was lurking under the abandoned tractor, shuddering each time the digger crashed and clanged through his old home. He had run out as soon as the builders had come into the barn, and had been hiding here ever since. He was wet, cold and hungry, and now he didn't even have anywhere to sleep!

As the barn was flattened, Ginger came to a decision. This wasn't his home any more. It hadn't been his home since his family had gone – he realized now that his mother wasn't coming back. He needed to get away, and find somewhere new.

Perhaps he could go and find that nice girl with the sandwiches?

Rosie's mum took her back to the farm on Sunday, and they stood by the fence calling for ages.

"Put some more cat treats down," Mum suggested. "Then at least he'll have something to eat."

Suddenly Rosie gasped. "Mum, look!"

"What is it? Have you spotted him? I can't see anything." Mum peered through the fence.

"No, that's it, I can't see anything, that's the point! The cat treats I poked through the fence on Friday, they've gone!"

"Are you sure?" Mum asked.

"Definitely. I was right here, so they should be just on the other side of the fence. Ginger's been here, he's eaten them! Oh, Mum!" Rosie beamed at her, feeling so relieved. She bent down to empty some more cat treats out of the packet.

"Rosie, what's that?" Rosie looked up to see her mum pointing across the farmyard, down to the side of the farmhouse. "Can you see? It looks like something ginger, by the bins…"

Rosie jumped to her feet. Mum was right. Slipping along the side of the farmhouse was a flash of gingery fur. It had to be him!

But then the creature slunk out further into the yard, sniffing at the piles of wood from the barn. A gingery fox, with a bright-white tail tip.

"Oh no…" Rosie breathed. It wasn't very big, but compared to a tiny kitten it was huge. "It might hurt Ginger, and oh, Mum, I bet it was the fox who ate the cat treats!"

Mum sighed and nodded. "I'm afraid it could well have been, yes."

Sadly, they turned and walked away, Rosie blinking back tears. She had promised herself she wouldn't give up, but it was starting to look hopeless…

That evening, Rosie's mum was determined to cheer her up. A television programme they both liked was just about to start and Mum hurried upstairs to fetch her.

"Rosie!" she called, opening her bedroom door. "Are you coming downstairs? Oh, Rosie!"

Rosie was sitting huddled on the floor, leaning against her bed.

"Whatever's the matter?" Mum asked, sitting down on the floor beside her. "You're crying!"

"I'll never see him again." Rosie sniffed. "What if he's hurt?" she whispered. "He might have been injured when the barn was knocked down. Maybe he got trapped somewhere. Maybe that fox has eaten him!" Tears rolled down Rosie's cheeks again.

"Ssshh, Rosie, don't say that." Mum hugged her close. "I don't think foxes normally attack cats. You're imagining the worst, the kitten might be fine. He's probably just staying hidden because he's frightened of the builders." She looked down, stroking Rosie's red hair. "You really love this kitten, don't you? You've tried so hard to make friends with him – Gran told me how patient you were, trying to get him to like you."

Rosie's mum hesitated. "Rosie, you know, we could try adopting one of the other kittens at the rescue centre… What about that pretty little black one?"

Rosie looked up, her eyes horrified and still teary. "We can't! We can't, Mum!"

"I mean, if we don't find Ginger," her mum explained gently.

Rosie shook her head. "He's special," she said in a quiet voice. "I think because he's ginger too, like me. But it isn't just that. He seems so bright, and he's got so much bounce…"

She twisted one of her red curls round her finger, deep in thought. It was true. Ginger *was* special. And if she couldn't have Ginger, she didn't want another kitten.

Chapter Six

Ginger had felt so brave when he decided to leave the farm and look for a new home. He had waited until all the people were long gone, and the farm was dark and quiet. He would find somewhere warm and comfortable. Maybe he'd even find that friendly girl with the food.

But he hadn't realized that the fence

went all round the farm. It was very high, and it was pinned down tight to the ground. He couldn't get out! Scratching and scrabbling at it didn't work, and when he tried climbing it he fell. At last he had slunk miserably away to find a place to sleep. He'd hidden himself eventually in Mrs Bowen's log-pile, at the back of the farmhouse. It wasn't very comfortable, but it felt safe, far away from the builders' noisy, smelly machines.

Most of the mice seemed to have been scared away by the men, too. He'd almost caught one once, but it had slipped into a hole at the last minute, leaving him worn out and hungrier than ever. It had seemed so easy when his mother did it. He'd found some rather fishy-tasting little round things by the fence over the last couple of days, but they hadn't filled him up. He'd seen a fox hanging around as well, and he had a feeling it had picked all the best bits out of those bin bags, because there was nothing left.

Now he could feel himself growing weaker. Even though the rain leaked through into his log-pile nest and soaked him, he'd been grateful for it, as at least he wasn't thirsty. He'd been able to lap the water caught in the old buckets that were lying around the yard. But he needed more than water. He was sure the men had food. He'd smelled it, delicious smells like the sandwiches the girl used to bring him. They had been very good.

He had hoped she might come back, but probably she didn't like the big machines either, he thought, as he drifted into a restless sleep.

Ginger was woken by the smell of ham sandwiches. A builder had stopped for lunch and was sitting on one of the big logs. The smell was irresistible. Ginger uncurled himself and crept out. The sandwiches were in an open box, lying next to the man. There was just one left, and out of it trailed a piece of wonderful pink ham. He had to have it. Ginger looked up at the man. He was staring across the yard, chewing slowly. He wouldn't notice, would he?

Ginger darted a paw into the box, hooking the bread with his claws.

"Hey! Get out of it, you!" The man swiped at him with his hand! Ginger shot away in terror, without even a morsel of bread to show for it. He raced up the tree that had been left standing in a corner of the yard by the fence, and crouched flat on one of the branches, quivering with terror. No one had ever tried to hit him before. He looked down fearfully, digging his claws into the bark. He had never climbed a tree before either, but instinct had taken him to the safest place. The man hadn't followed him.

Ginger stayed there for hours, too scared to move. By the middle of the afternoon, he felt it might be safe to come down from the tree. It wasn't as easy as going up had been. He hadn't really *thought* about going up, he'd just done it. He looked down from his branch – the ground seemed so far away… He was stuck!

Rosie only got through school that day because Millie kept nudging her, reminding her that Mrs Wilkinson was watching. Rosie would manage to listen or concentrate on what she was supposed to be doing for about five minutes, before she started thinking about Ginger again.

Millie was coming back to Gran's for tea today, and they were planning to look for Ginger together. Rosie was glad – Millie was so enthusiastic about looking for him. Rosie had been disappointed so many times, it was hard to keep her hopes up.

Millie jogged ahead as they came up to the farm. "Wow! It really is a building site. Oh, Rosie, poor Ginger. He must be really scared with all those people around, and those great big diggers. It's so noisy!"

Rosie nodded sadly and looked wearily through the fence into the farmyard. It looked so different now, with the barn gone and the yard covered in piles of rubble. She wasn't expecting to see anything. But what was that in the big tree over there? Rosie peered through the wire fence and grabbed Millie's sleeve.

"Millie! Gran! Look! Is that a cat in

the tree? On that branch, there. No, no, there, look!"

A flash of ginger fur showed among the yellowing leaves. It was hard to see if it was a cat, but *something* was moving.

"You could be right…" Millie murmured doubtfully. "I can't quite see."

Gran was squinting through the fence at the tree. "I can't tell either…"

"I am right! I know I am!" Rosie looked at them eagerly. "He's there, he really is. Yes, I can see his stripes! Oh, I can't believe it, I'd almost given up. Ginger! Ginger! I don't think he can hear me, with all this noise." She frowned. "Oh, Gran, he must be so scared with all this going on. We have to get him out, we just have to!"

She dashed along the fence to the gate, with Millie racing after her, and shouted to one of the men walking by. "Hey! Excuse me! Over here, please listen!"

But the man just walked past, trundling a wheelbarrow. He didn't even look at Rosie and Millie. Rosie rattled the gate, but no one seemed to hear her, the site was too noisy.

Gran came up, looking anxious. "Rosie, calm down!"

"I can't make anyone listen!" Rosie looked at her wildly. "They have to let us in so we can go and get him!"

Gran pulled them gently away from the gate. "Girls, come back, it's a building site, I don't think they'll let us go in. Sshh, look, that man's coming out. We'll ask him." Gran smiled politely at the builder, who was giving them a curious look.

"Excuse me, but have you seen a ginger kitten around at all? He used to live on the farm, and he's disappeared. We think we might have just seen him in that tree."

The builder shook his head. He didn't look very interested. "No cats, sorry," he said, starting to shut the gate.

"He *is* there!" Rosie cried. "We've just seen him, we know he's there. You've knocked down his home, you might've hurt him! You have to let us find him!"

The builder looked confused, and Gran hugged Rosie tight. "Calm down, Rosie. Look, I'm sorry, the girls are very worried about the kitten. We really do think we saw him a minute ago. Could you please just keep an eye out for him?" She pulled an old till receipt out of her bag and scribbled on it. "This is my phone number. If you could call us if you see him, we'd be so grateful."

The man took the note and stuffed it into the pocket of his reflective vest. Then he locked the gate, and walked off. Rosie watched him go, tears running down her nose. She was pretty sure he'd never look at the note again.

Gran shepherded Rosie and Millie away from the gate. She was worried the builders might get annoyed and tell them to stop hanging around.

From high up in the tree, Ginger had heard the voices. It was the girl! The one with the food, who did the stroking. She'd come back for him. He was sure that was why she was there. He tried desperately to scrabble down the tree trunk.

But now she was going! She couldn't have seen him. He mewed frantically, *please wait!* But no one heard him. He took a flying leap from halfway down the tree trunk, and raced over to the fence.

Come back! Come back! I'm here!

But it was too late.

Chapter Seven

When they got back to Gran's house, she made Millie and Rosie sit down and have a glass of juice.

"You mustn't get so het up, Rosie!" Gran said. "You can't help that kitten if you're shouting at people and getting into trouble, can you?"

Rosie sighed and shook her head. Gran was right. "I just don't think he was even listening, Gran," she said sadly. "That's why I was so cross. That man just said no cats, without even thinking about it!"

"But you saw him, Rosie!" Millie put in. "He's still there, that's really good news! That was your ginger kitten, wasn't it?"

Rosie smiled at last. "I'm sure, really sure. It was his lovely stripy fur, I could see it through the leaves. He was up in that tree, I know he was. I wish he'd heard me, but it was just so noisy. I bet he would have come down, to see if I had sandwiches again." She frowned. "I hope he wasn't stuck, that tree's enormous."

"Well, all we can do is go again tomorrow. As long as we're back in time for your mum to pick you up, I don't mind how long we stay. If we're there when the builders have gone and it's quiet, then it'll be easier." Gran smiled. "If he's there, we'll find him."

"Couldn't we go back now?" Rosie pleaded. "I'm not sure I can wait until tomorrow…"

Gran shook her head. "It's getting late now and you both still need to have your tea. We can go straight after school tomorrow."

"OK," Rosie sighed.

Ginger sat by the fence and howled. She'd been here, and he'd missed her! He scratched desperately at the fence, hoping to chase after the girl, but it didn't budge at all. He was still trapped.

He trailed sadly back to the woodpile, avoiding the builders. At least she had come back. Maybe she'd come again tomorrow?

Rosie raced along the lane, hardly hearing Gran calling to her to slow down. She was desperate to get to the farm, and see if Ginger was still there. At last she reached the fence by the tree, where Ginger had been yesterday. She wound her fingers through the wire, gazing hopefully up at the tree. There was no glint of ginger fur. Rosie sighed. Still, she couldn't expect him to be in exactly the same place he was yesterday, that would be silly.

He's there, she told herself firmly. *You just need to look.*

Rosie tiptoed along the fence, trying to peer through. The awful thing was, Ginger might be asleep somewhere, just out of sight! She could miss him so easily.

Suddenly Rosie gasped. It was as though all her breath had disappeared. He was there! Keeping so still that she hadn't spotted him. He was crouched under the massive wheel of the old tractor, where she used to sit to tempt him with sandwiches. His ears were laid back, and he was watching the builders. Rosie's heart thudded miserably as she saw how thin he was getting.

Rosie crouched down by the fence. "Ginger!" she whispered, not wanting to scare him, but of course he didn't hear her. She tried again, a little louder, and his ears twitched.

"Ginger!" Rosie waved to him as well this time, and she saw his eyes widen. He'd seen her! He stood up slowly, cautiously, and crept across the yard towards her, moving one paw at a time and glancing around fearfully.

Rosie's eyes filled with tears as she saw how scared he was. "Hey, Ginger!" she whispered gently, as he stopped a metre or so from the fence.

He stood hesitantly, staring at her, and gave a very small mew. Had the girl come back for him?

"Oh, Ginger, I'm so glad to see you!" Rosie murmured. "Are you all right? You look OK, just really thin." She giggled. "I don't know why I'm asking you all these questions, it isn't as if you can answer..." Very slowly, Rosie reached into her school bag. "Look, I've got your favourite..." She opened up her lunch box, pulling out the sandwiches she'd saved. "Yummy ham, Ginger, come and see!"

Ginger ran towards her. She *had* come back! And she'd brought food. He was still nervous, but she'd always been so gentle, and the food just smelled too good to resist. Although he was half wild, he'd been used to Rosie feeding him from when he was quite tiny, and he'd missed her. He sat on the other side of the fence and meowed hopefully.

"Here you go, it's OK," Rosie said, laughing and posting pieces of sandwich through the fence. Ginger gobbled them down eagerly. "You look like you haven't eaten for a week," Rosie told him. Her eyes widened. "Actually, it *is* a week, isn't it? You must be starved. Here, have some more."

"Rosie, I can't believe you've already found him! I won't come closer in case I frighten him off, all right? I'll just stay back here." Gran leaned against the fence on the other side of the lane, watching Rosie and the kitten.

Ginger finished the sandwich, and sniffed the ground, looking for crumbs. The sandwich had helped, but he still felt hungry. He wondered if the girl had any more. He looked at her uncertainly, and edged forward, closer and closer still. At last he was right up against the fence, sniffing at Rosie's fingers. He even licked them, in case she tasted of ham, but she didn't.

Rosie giggled – his tongue was tickly – and scratched him behind the ears. She could only just reach – the holes in the fence were too small for her whole hand to go through. "How are we going to get you out?" Rosie muttered, as she stroked Ginger's head with one finger.

He ducked his head shyly, rubbing himself against the wire. It was warm and sunny, he had been fed, and now someone he liked was fussing over him.

He closed his eyes, and started to purr, very quietly, his tiny chest buzzing.

Rosie could feel him trembling with the purr as he leaned against the wire, letting her stroke him all over. She almost felt like purring herself, and a huge smile spread over her face.

"He's purring!" she hissed to Gran in a loud whisper. Rosie was just starting to wonder if she should call to a nearby builder, and ask him to pick Ginger up and bring him out to her. It wouldn't take him long, and they couldn't *want* a kitten getting in their way…

Then the man tripped and dropped the bucket he was carrying. It hit the ground with a huge clang. Ginger leaped into the air in fright, and Rosie jumped, her heart thumping.

Ginger had disappeared, streaking across the yard in a panic, and Rosie looked anxiously around for him, clinging sadly on to the wire fence. He had trusted her – he'd actually been enjoying her stroking him, and now all that good work was for nothing!

She sighed hopelessly. Ginger was so nervous. It wasn't his fault, but he was never going to let one of the builders pick him up. He'd run away from the girls from the rescue centre, and that was before he'd had a week of scary builders invading his home.

Ginger would let her feed him, and stroke him. But she was on one side of the fence, and he was on the other. How was she ever going to get him out?

Chapter Eight

"Oh, Rosie, he was so close!" Gran came hurrying over, her face stricken. "That was such bad luck. He really seemed to be trusting you." She shook her head. "I just can't believe how patient you've been with him. You deserve to have him, Rosie, you really do."

Rosie gave her a grateful hug.

"Well, what are we going to do now?" Gran wondered. "How on earth are we going to get him out? He's too frightened to let anyone pick him up – you might just about be able to do it, but those builders can't let you go on to the site, even if they want to. If you hurt yourself, they could be in real trouble. I suppose we're just going to have to call the rescue centre and get them to do it."

Rosie nodded. "I hadn't thought of the rescue centre people coming back. They'd probably have to use a net or a cage or something, wouldn't they?" She shuddered. "I suppose it's better than staying where he is, it's really dangerous here. But he'll be terrified and he might run away from them again...

Oh, Gran, there's got to be a better way!" She sat down on the grassy verge, thinking hard. "Well, I can't go in, so he's got to come out, hasn't he? But I just don't see how – this fence is like a prison, even for a cat."

Gran sighed. "I've a feeling we're going to be here for a while, aren't we?" She patted Rosie on the shoulder. "You stay here and watch for him, I'll nip home and make us some sandwiches. I won't be long." Rosie looked up suddenly. "Don't worry, Rosie, I'll bring some more ham for Ginger as well. But if we do catch that kitten, he's going to have to learn to like something other than the best ham…"

Rosie watched her walk slowly off down the lane. She was so lucky having Gran. For a start, if Gran didn't have her after school, she'd never even have met Ginger. But mostly because Gran was never in a rush. She didn't mind spending an hour sitting outside a building site, watching for a kitten. That was pretty special.

Rosie turned back to the fence and stared at it hopelessly. If only she could climb over it! The builders were starting to leave now. Once they'd gone, no one would see... But the fence was so high, and Gran would be really upset with her. She'd trusted Rosie to be sensible, leaving her here. Rosie couldn't let her down.

Rosie shook the fence, making it rattle. It was even taller than the one at school, round the playing field. Then she stopped, and stared at the fence thoughtfully. The one at school had holes in, where people had leaned on it over the years, and one place where some of the boys in the year above had decided to dig a tunnel underneath while they were bored in lunch break.

She couldn't get *over* the fence, but maybe she could get *under* it. Or at least the kitten could…

She crouched down again and peered at the base of the fence. It ran along the ground, and it was held tightly between posts, so there were no gaps – yet. Rosie started to hunt for a likely place. Oh! Yes, here, a couple of posts along… Something had already done half the job for her. Maybe that fox they'd seen before. Whatever it was had scrabbled a hole a few centimetres deep under the fence before it gave up.

Rosie lifted the fence carefully. She was pretty sure that Ginger could fit under there, but she'd better dig it out a bit more, just to be certain. Rosie found a big stone and started to scrape the earth away as fast as she could, looking up every so often to check for Ginger.

The farm was quiet. Ginger's ears and whiskers stopped their panicky twitching at last, and he poked his nose out from under the black tarpaulin where he'd dashed after that huge bang.

No noise of diggers, no rumbling wheels, no men shouting. They had gone. It should be safe now. He slid out, still listening carefully. There was an odd scritch-scratching noise coming from across the yard. It wasn't the men. Was it that fox who'd been stealing from his bins? He'd seen it again the other night.

There was no smell now, so it couldn't be a fox. He padded slowly out into the yard, following the noise. It sounded like something was digging under the fence, maybe it *was* that fox. The fur rose up on Ginger's back. The sooner he got out of here, the better. He crept round the back of the tractor, and darted a quick look over at the fence.

It was her! The girl! She was still there! The noise hadn't scared her away. And she was digging under the fence. Was she trying to come in?

Ginger gave a hopeful mew, and crept across the yard towards her, glancing round occasionally, just in case.

Rosie dropped the stone. "Ginger!" She sat up on her heels eagerly, catching hold of the fence to look through the wire, and Ginger paused, scared by the sudden movement. "Oh, I'm sorry…" She edged back on her knees, leaving a little space between herself and the fence. "I didn't mean to scare you, Ginger. I was just so glad to see you! Look!" Rosie dug the last tiny handful of fishy cat treats out of the packet that she'd been keeping in her school bag, and scattered them for Ginger – on her side of the fence.

"Come on, Ginger… Please…"

The tiny kitten sniffed thoughtfully. The smell was familiar. Those strange round things he'd found before! They were from the girl, too? Well, he preferred ham sandwiches, but he wouldn't complain. Still, he had to climb under the fence to get them.

He padded closer, peering through the hole. It seemed big enough. And he'd been hoping to find the girl, and a way out. Now she had made him one. Ginger stared up at Rosie, his big green eyes hopeful, and almost trusting. He would do it.

Rosie stared back, her eyes hopeful too, and pleading, desperate for him to trust her. "Hey, little one," she whispered. "Come on…"

Ginger crouched down, and started to wriggle under the fence, the wire just skimming the fur on his back. He popped out the other side, shook himself and sneezed from the dust. Then he eyed the cat treats, eagerly.

"Go on, they're for you!" Rosie reassured him, and Ginger gobbled them down, a curious expression on his face. Such an odd flavour. But he could get used to it. He licked his whiskers to make sure he hadn't missed anything, and looked up at Rosie. Then he put one tiny paw on her knee, and mewed.

More?

"Are you still hungry?" Rosie smiled. "You could come back to Gran's with me... She's making ham sandwiches, your favourite." She stood up, very slowly, and stepped backwards. "You coming? Hmmm? Coming, Ginger?"

And Ginger stepped out after her, his tail waving, following her home.

Misty the Abandoned Kitten

For Tabitha

Chapter One

Amy yawned and rolled over to go back to sleep. But then she stopped halfway and bounced up in bed. It was her birthday! Was it too early to go and wake up Mum and Dad? Amy grabbed her watch off the bedside table. Half-past six. Surely that was late enough, on a birthday?

Shivering slightly in the chill

morning, she threw on her dressing gown, and hurried along the landing to her parents' room.

"Oh! Amy... Happy Birthday..." Her dad yawned hugely. "Is it as early as it feels?"

"It's already half-past six," Amy replied. "Can't we get up? Please, Mum?"

Her mum was already starting to climb out of bed. "You'd better go and get dressed."

"OK!" Amy grinned. She dashed back to her room and started to put on her school uniform, sighing a little. It was so unfair to have to go to school on her birthday. Still, as she was up early, at least Mum might let her open some of her presents...

Amy ran down the stairs eagerly and

burst into the kitchen.

"Oh, wow!" she said, as she sat down at the table in front of a pile of birthday presents. She smiled as she saw that her mum had draped fairy lights round the window. "That looks fab!"

"Well, since you've got to go to school, I thought I'd try and make breakfast special." Amy's mum put a chocolate croissant in front of her.

Just then, Dad came into the kitchen. "I hope there's one for me too," he said, giving Amy a hug. "Happy Birthday!"

"Go on, open your presents," her mum said, smiling.

Amy reached out for the nearest parcel, which was enticingly squashy.

"Oh, it's lovely. Gran's so clever!" she said, as she tore off the paper and shook out a purple hoodie top, with a pink satin cat stitched on to the back, and glittery stars all around.

Her mum smiled. "I told her anything with a cat on it."

When Amy had finally unwrapped all her presents, her dad shook his head. "Do you know, anyone would think you liked cats!" he remarked, staring at the cat T-shirt, cat lunch box, kitten pencil case, and the gorgeous toy Persian cat on Amy's lap. Her mum and dad knew how much she loved cats. But they just didn't think she was old enough to have one as a pet, however much she begged.

"Come on, we need to get to school," Mum pointed out. "I've arranged for you to go for tea at Lily's today, Amy."

Amy looked up in surprise. It was the first she'd heard about this.

Her dad winked. "I need a bit of extra time to sort out your surprise present from us. Didn't you notice we haven't given you anything yet? It'll be waiting for you when you get home."

"Oh!" Amy beamed at him. That sounded really exciting…

"Do you think the surprise could be a kitten?" Amy asked Lily, for about the fifteenth time that day. The girls had finished their tea and had gone up to Lily's room to chat.

Her best friend sighed. "I *still* don't know! Did it sound like they'd changed their minds the last time you asked?"

Amy shook her head. "Mum said I wasn't old enough to look after a pet properly. I told her you do!"

Lily smiled and stroked Stella, her big tabby cat, who was curled up on the duvet between them. "I was lucky. Mum loves cats. I didn't have to beg!"

"Dad could have needed the time to go and fetch a kitten." Amy was thinking aloud. "I can't think of anything else it would be. Oh, I just don't know!" She leaned down so she was nose to nose with Stella, who stared back at her sleepily. "I wish you could tell me. Am I getting a kitten at last?"

Stella yawned, showing all her teeth.

"Hmmm. I'm not sure what that means." Amy sighed. "Oh! Is that the doorbell?" she exclaimed, scrambling to her feet.

Lily frowned. "It's rude to be so happy about going home!" She laughed at Amy's suddenly worried face. "I'm only teasing! Go! Go on! I've got all my fingers crossed for you! Call and tell me if it *is* a kitten!"

A few streets away, a little black kitten was sitting in a cardboard carrier, mewing sadly. She didn't like it in here, and things didn't smell right. She wanted to go back to her lovely home.

"Sshh, sshh, Jet." There was a scuffling noise at the top of the box, and the kitten looked up nervously. "Let's get you out, little one."

The kitten pressed herself into the corner as the dark box opened up. Then she gave a squeak of relief. There was her owner!

Mrs Jones reached in and gently lifted out the little cat. She lowered herself down into an armchair and the kitten curled up on her lap.

"Can we play with Jet, Gran?" Two children had followed Mrs Jones into the room. "Please!" the little girl squealed.

"Millie, calm down!" Mrs Jones said firmly. "You'll scare her."

The kitten looked up at the children, both reaching out for her, and squirmed into Mrs Jones's cardigan.

"I just want to stroke her," the little boy begged.

"I'm sorry, Dan. I know you both want to say hello, but she's only just arrived, and she's not really used to being with children. She'll soon settle in, I'm sure, and then you can play with her all you want."

"Don't bother Gran, you two. You know she needs to rest and get better." The children's mother was standing in the doorway now. "Do you want a cup of tea or anything, Mum?"

"No, no, Sarah, thank you. I'm just going to sit here with Jet to keep me company."

"OK. Come on, you two. Don't forget to shut the door – you know we need to keep Jet in here for the next few days."

The children ran off after their mum, and the kitten relaxed. This place wasn't home, but at least Mrs Jones was here.

"Oh dear, it's a big change, isn't it?" The old lady tickled her under the chin. "Still, Sarah's right. I'm better off here where she can keep an eye on me."

But Jet wasn't listening. She'd tensed up again, the fur on her tiny black tail bristling. Millie and Dan hadn't shut the door properly after all, and there was another cat here. A big Siamese staring at her with round blue eyes. She mewed anxiously. Did this house already belong to another cat?

Mrs Jones looked over at the cat. "Oh, there's Charlie. Don't worry, Jet. He's friendly; Sarah told me he'd be no trouble. No trouble at all."

"Come out into the garden!" Amy's dad held open the back door, an excited expression on his face.

"The present is outside?" Amy asked doubtfully. Why would a kitten be outside? She stepped out, and looked round at her parents, who were beaming at her.

"Look at the tree!" Dad pointed up at the big chestnut tree at the end of the garden.

"Oh! A tree house!" Amy said, sounding rather surprised.

"Don't you like it?" Her dad's voice was suddenly anxious.

"Yes, I do, I love it." Amy hugged him. It was true – she had always wanted a little private hideaway of her own. It was just that it wasn't a kitten…

"Why don't you go and explore?" said Mum.

Amy ran down the garden and climbed the wooden ladder that her dad had fastened on to the tree trunk.

The tree house smelled lovely, of new wood. Amy looked round it delightedly. There was a big purple beanbag to sit on, and on a tiny wooden table by the square window was a birthday cake, with pink icing.

Amy leaned out of the door, and smiled down at her parents. "It's a brilliant present. Thank you!"

"We'll cut the cake in about half an hour, OK?" said Mum, smiling.

Amy sat down on the beanbag, and sighed. She loved the tree house – but at the same time, she was secretly a little disappointed. "I should have known it wouldn't be a kitten," she whispered to herself. "It was just that I was really hoping…"

Chapter Two

On Saturday it was Amy's birthday party. She and Lily and a couple of other friends from school were going to the cinema, and then to her favourite café for tea. She was really looking forward to it – but every so often something would remind her about kittens and she'd feel sad again.

"I can never decide whether to have sweet or salty popcorn," said Lily, as she and Amy walked over to the food counter. "Or do you want to share some pick 'n' mix instead? Amy…?" She turned to her friend. "Are you OK? You seem a bit quiet," she whispered. "Is it about your present?"

Amy nodded. "My tree house is really cool. I can't wait for you to see it." She sighed. "Maybe they'll change their minds about me getting a cat in time for my next birthday."

Lily gave her a hug. "You can come and borrow Stella any time."

Amy smiled at her gratefully, but it wasn't the same as a kitten of her own.

Mrs Jones's daughter, Sarah, had promised her that Charlie would be fine with having another cat in the house. She was really worried about her mum, who'd had a couple of bad falls, and she wanted to be able to look after her. And that meant her kitten, too. But Sarah just hadn't realized how jealous Charlie would be.

"Come on! Auntie Grace says she's made a cake!" The children were struggling into their coats, and Sarah was trying to hurry everyone up. It was Sunday, and all the family were going over to visit Mrs Jones's other daughter.

Jet heard the front door bang, Mrs Jones's stick tapping as she went down the front step and then the noise of the children growing fainter as they walked down the path. They were all going out! Jet shivered. She was hiding under a bookshelf in the living room. It was very low to the ground and she'd discovered that Charlie couldn't chase her under there, as he was too big. It wasn't a very nice place to stay – it was dusty and she had to lie flat to fit – but at least it was safe.

Now that she was allowed out of the living room and into the rest of the house, Jet spent almost the whole time hiding from Charlie. He kept pouncing on her, and he was a lot bigger than she was. They had been sharing the house properly for almost a week now, and he hadn't got any better. He kept stealing her food, too, so she was hungry all the time. But he was sneaky enough only to do it when no one was looking. If the family were there he would just glare at her until she felt too scared to eat and slunk away from her bowl.

Jet couldn't see him now, though. Perhaps he'd gone out of the cat flap into the garden? Nervously, she edged only her whiskers out of her hiding place and waited. She risked a paw out, then another, then squirmed forwards, her heart racing. No, he wasn't there. She was safe.

She was terribly hungry, though. Charlie had chased her away from her breakfast that morning, and she really wanted to go to the kitchen and see if he'd left anything. With her whiskers trembling and her tail fluffed up, the kitten crept out into the hallway, and dashed to the kitchen door, where she did another careful search. She couldn't see him anywhere. And there was some food left! Gratefully, she scampered over to her bowl, and started to gulp down the cat biscuits.

Behind her, on one of the kitchen chairs, hidden by the plastic tablecloth, a long chocolate-brown tail began to twitch slowly back and forth.

Jet was so absorbed in wolfing what was left of her breakfast that she didn't hear the thud as Charlie's paws hit the floor. But some sense of danger made her whiskers prickle, and she turned round just as he flung himself at her. She shot away, scooting across the kitchen floor and making a dive for the cat flap. She batted at it desperately with her nose and scrambled through, racing across the garden to hide under a bush.

Huddled against the damp leaves, she watched the cat flap swing a couple of times. Charlie wasn't following her. Probably because he was eating the rest of her breakfast, Jet thought miserably.

What should she do? She hadn't explored the garden much until now –

she'd always stayed close to Mrs Jones, or hidden herself somewhere in the house. Jet poked her nose out from under the bush, sniffing the crisp morning air. It was chilly – too chilly to sit still. But she didn't want to go back inside, not with Charlie about. Instead, she set off down the garden, sniffing at the bird seed that had fallen out of the bird feeders, and cautiously inspecting the scooters and toys that the children had left lying around.

Nervously, she checked behind her, to make sure Charlie hadn't sneaked through the cat flap. Just then, a fat blackbird swooped past her nose, and she pricked up her ears in astonishment. She wasn't really used to being in the garden, and birds were new and exciting.

She swished through the long grass, almost glad now that Charlie had chased her outside. The blackbird swooped and dived in and out of the plants by the fence, and the kitten trotted after it. Then it disappeared.

Surprised, she looked around, trying to work out where it had gone. That was when she noticed the hole. There was a big gap under the fence, leading into the next-door garden. This would be a perfect way to get away from Charlie. She had been looking back every so often, to check that he wasn't following, but if she went into a different garden, he would never find her! Pleased with her plan, the kitten slipped underneath the fence, and set off to explore.

Early that Sunday morning, Amy disappeared up into her tree house, taking the book she had to read for school. It was a chilly morning for April, so she was wearing her new hoodie from Gran, and a pink fluffy scarf and hat. But even though it was cold, being up in the tree house felt wonderful.

It wasn't really all that high up, but it was such fun looking down on the gardens from her hideaway amongst the leaves. The chestnut tree was right at the end of their long, thin garden, but she could just see Mum moving around in the kitchen. Amy moved the beanbag so that it was in the doorway and flumped down on it, watching a blackbird hopping around in next-door's flower bed. There was an early morning mist hanging over the grass, and it felt quite spooky – just right for her book, which was a ghost story.

Amy read a few pages. She was just getting to a scary bit when a strange rustling noise outside made her jump. A little movement by the garden fence caught her eye, and Amy peered down. It was a little black kitten! She was half-wreathed in mist, and for a second Amy wondered if this was a ghost-cat. She caught her breath in excitement, watching as the tiny thing nosed her way through the plants and spotted the blackbird, who was still pecking about in the grass on the other side of the garden.

The kitten settled into a hunting crouch, her tail whisking from side to side, and wriggled forwards on to the lawn. Amy giggled. This was no ghost! The kitten was so funny, stalking across the grass like a tiny panther. The bird spotted her at once, hopping up on to the fence and squawking crossly.

The kitten turned away and began to play with a leaf instead, as though she'd never even thought of chasing the bird.

Amy was just wondering whether, if she climbed down quietly, the kitten would let her stroke it, when the little creature suddenly darted back the way she'd come – under the fence and into the mists of next-door's garden.

Amy watched the shadowy little figure disappear. "I wonder who she belongs to?" she whispered to herself. "And what her name is. If I could get close enough, I could look on her collar, maybe." Then she frowned. "No, I don't think she had one. I think I'd call her Misty." She put her chin in her hands, and imagined a little black kitten curled up on the end of her bed. "I can't wait to tell Lily about her!"

Chapter Three

"Have you seen her again?" Lily asked eagerly, and Amy smiled.

"Yesterday, just as I was going out into the garden. She was sitting on the back fence, right under the tree house. But when I got closer she ran off."

"You've seen her a few times now. Maybe she lives in one of the houses close by," Lily suggested.

Amy frowned. "She doesn't have a collar, though. I just wonder – perhaps she's a stray? She never comes very close – I think she's quite shy of people. A stray kitten could be like that, couldn't it?"

Lily nodded thoughtfully.

"And she looks ever so thin," Amy added. "I'm worried she isn't getting enough food."

"Poor little thing!" Lily cried. "Kittens do need to eat a lot. Or she might just be naturally skinny. Kittens can be. Oh, I wish I could see her."

"If we're lucky she might turn up when you come to tea on Friday," Amy said. Lily was a cat expert and might be able to think of a way she could help the kitten.

By now the little kitten was exploring the gardens all along the road. She had discovered that she loved being outside – there were always new and exciting things to play with. Sometimes people left food out, too. Even if it was only stale bread meant for the birds, it was better than nothing, as Charlie was still stealing most of her meals. She'd got very good at scrambling up bird tables. She wasn't as good at chasing the birds themselves – somehow they always seemed to work out that she was coming. But she enjoyed trying.

Being outside was definitely better than being at her new house, anyway. Even when Charlie left her alone, which wasn't often, Mrs Jones's two grandchildren were almost as bad. They liked to fuss over her and stroke her, which the kitten didn't mind too much. And sometimes it was quite fun to chase the string that they dangled in front of her nose. But they also kept trying to pick her up, which she hated, especially as they just grabbed her and hauled her along with her legs dangling, even though Mrs Jones had explained how to hold her properly. The kitten tried to stay out of their way.

"Puss! Puss, puss, puss! Where are you, Jet?" Millie called.

The kitten slipped quickly under the kitchen table, but it was an obvious hiding place, and the little girl crawled underneath to be with her. Jet's tail started to twitch nervously.

Millie was carrying a handful of dolls' clothes, but she dropped them on the floor and seized the kitten round her middle.

Jet yowled, wriggling desperately to get away, but the little girl held her firmly. Millie then grabbed a doll's jacket and started trying to place one of her paws into it. "You're going to look so pretty! Charlie's too big for all my dolls' clothes, but you're just the right size."

The kitten scrabbled frantically and raked her tiny claws across Millie's hand. The little girl dropped Jet in surprise, and the kitten shot out from under the table, and cowered in the corner of the kitchen, hissing furiously.

Millie howled, staring at the red scratch across the back of her hand.

"What happened?" Sarah ran into the kitchen, and Millie scrambled out from under the table. "Jet hurt me!" she wailed, holding out her hand.

"Jet did that?" Sarah turned to stare at the kitten. "Bad cat! You mustn't scratch people!" She sounded really cross, and the kitten slunk guiltily out of the kitchen to find Mrs Jones, knowing that she would understand.

Mrs Jones was in her favourite armchair as usual. But Charlie was there too. Curled up cosily on Mrs Jones's lap, looking as though he belonged there. Just where the kitten was meant to be.

Mrs Jones was dozing, and she didn't see Jet, staring wide-eyed from the corner of the room. The kitten watched for only a second, then she ran back the way she'd come, past Millie still sobbing in the kitchen, and straight out of the cat flap.

Charlie wasn't only taking her food now – he was taking Mrs Jones too.

Amy was up in the tree house, sitting by the door and looking out over the garden. She was drawing in the beautiful sketchbook that one of her aunts had given her for her birthday, with a set of new pencils too. She was trying to remember exactly what that gorgeous little kitten had looked like. She wished she had seen her closer up – she still wasn't sure exactly what colour her eyes were. She hesitated between the two greens in her new pencil box. Probably the lighter one. Smiling to herself, she finished colouring the eyes, and wrote *Misty* in the bottom corner of the page.

Every time she went up to her tree house, Amy watched out for the kitten, but she hadn't seen her for a couple of days. Maybe she had a home after all?

It was just as Amy was admitting to herself that the kitten might not come back, that she saw her again. She was walking carefully along the fence that ran across the back of Amy's garden – almost underneath the tree house. Amy caught her breath. She watched as the little creature padded along the narrow boards of the fence, like a tightrope walker. She smiled proudly to herself, noting that she had made the kitten's eyes exactly the right colour.

"Puss, puss, puss…" she called, very gently and quietly.

The kitten looked up, startled. She had been watching a white butterfly and hadn't seen the girl at all. She tensed up, ready to run. This girl was calling her like Millie had – was she going to try and pull her about, or dress her up in dolls' clothes?

But the girl didn't move. She was sitting up in a strange little house in a tree. Her voice was different too. Quieter. She didn't make the kitten feel nervous, like Dan and Millie did.

The girl moved, and the kitten stepped back a pace, wondering if she should leap down from the fence and race across the garden to safety – although she wasn't quite sure where that was, now that Mrs Jones wasn't hers any more.

But the girl didn't try to grab her. She just shifted herself so that she was perched on the ladder, her arm trailing down. The kitten looked up. If she stretched, she could just brush the girl's fingers with the side of her face. She could mark the girl with her scent. Her whiskers bristled with surprise at the idea that she might make this girl belong to her. She took a step closer, and then another, so that she could sniff the girl's fingers.

Swiftly, daringly, the kitten nudged the girl's hand. Then she leaped down from the fence and dashed back across the garden.

Chapter Four

Amy laughed delightedly to herself, as she watched the little kitten scurrying away. She could still feel the cold smudge of its nose against her hand.

"She came back!" she whispered happily to herself. She gazed down at her drawing and sighed. Misty was so much prettier in real life. Amy was sure she was a girl kitten, she was so delicate looking. Her fur was midnight-black and glossy, not the dull black of a drawing. She was very thin, though. Amy thought that she might even be thinner than when she'd seen her last week. If Misty was getting thinner, did that mean she didn't have an owner? Perhaps she'd got lost – Amy couldn't imagine anyone abandoning such a beautiful kitten. How could they?

If she was a stray... Amy played with her hair thoughtfully. She knew her mum and dad had said she was too young to look after a cat, and that if she told them she'd found a stray kitten, they would want to take it to the cat shelter. But now she had the tree house. Her own special, secret place. A perfect little house to hide a kitten in.

Amy shook her head and sighed. It was only a silly dream. But dreaming was fun…

"Guess what happened yesterday!" said Amy to Lily, as soon as their mums had said goodbye at the school gates. She grabbed her friend's hand and towed her over to a bench in a quiet corner of the playground.

"What?" Lily's eyes sparkled excitedly.

"The kitten came back again and I touched her! She came walking along our back fence when I was up in the tree house. She was really shy, but she sniffed my fingers, and sort of nudged me, you know how cats do?"

Lily nodded. "Stella does that, it's really sweet. Oh, I'm so glad I'm coming to your house tonight, maybe I'll see her too."

"The thing is, I definitely think she's got thinner since I last saw her." Amy sighed. "I'm really worried about her." She looked up at Lily. "Do you think I should feed her? I know she might belong to someone else, but I just don't see how she can. She's awfully thin."

Lily was practically bouncing up and down on the bench. "You should! You have to! But what are you going to feed her *on*?"

Amy smiled. "When you come home with me tonight, do you think you could ask to stop at the pet shop so you can buy some cat treats for Stella? I've brought some of my birthday money."

Lily nodded eagerly. "Of course. Stella really likes the salmon ones, we should get those."

Amy laughed. "I'm not sure this kitten would care about the flavour as long as it's food."

"I'll tell your mum I need a couple of extra tins of cat food, too," Lily added. "You can't just feed her on the treats."

"That would be brilliant," Amy told her gratefully.

"I can't wait to see her – can we go up in the tree house tonight and wait to see if she comes?"

Amy nodded. "I thought maybe if I put some food out, she might smell it."

"Good idea. We definitely need to get the fishy flavours then, they stink! My mum won't buy the tuna and prawn cat food, she says it makes her feel sick! A hungry kitten would smell it a mile off, I should think. Oh, Amy, this is so exciting." Lily gave her a hug. "It's almost like you're going to have your own cat after all!"

"She might not come," Amy said cautiously, but she hugged Lily back, unable to keep the smile off her face.

"You definitely want this kind!" Lily took a foil pouch of cat snacks from the shelf. "They smell really strong. The kitten won't be able to resist them." She placed the cat treats in her basket. "I've just thought, you'll have to give her a name. What are you going to call her?"

"I named her the first time I saw her," Amy admitted. "She's called Misty. Because I saw her coming towards me out of the mist, you see." She picked up a different packet of cat treats and added them to Lily's basket.

"Let's get these too – if this cat on the front was a kitten, it would look exactly like Misty."

"Very, very cute," Lily said.

"She is." Amy nodded. "I really hope she comes back this afternoon so you can see her! Oh, look, Mum's waving at us to hurry up." Amy's mum was waiting outside the pet shop for them.

"Goodness, you needed a lot of cat food!" she said to Lily, as the girls came out of the shop.

Lily giggled. "Stella is very greedy," she said, winking at Amy, or trying to; she wasn't very good at it, and had to screw up her face.

"Lily, are you all right?" Amy's mum asked. "Is there something in your eye?"

Amy burst out laughing, and her mum shook her head. "You two – sometimes I think it's a good thing I don't know what you're up to."

Amy and Lily grinned at each other. Secrets were such fun – and this was definitely the best one they had ever had.

They sneaked the cat food out into the garden while Amy's mum was preparing their tea.

"Wow!" Lily looked up at the tree house. "Your dad built that? He's brilliant!"

"It's cool, isn't it?" Amy agreed.

Lily hauled herself up the ladder and gazed around the inside of the tree house, admiring the bookshelf and the big purple beanbag.

"Come on, let's open these." Amy tore at the foil packet of cat treats eagerly. "I thought we could spread them out along the branch that almost touches the fence. I'm pretty sure Misty could jump on to it."

Amy carefully leaned out of the doorway to sprinkle some cat treats on to the wide branch below. "Now we need to wait," she said, edging backwards. She emptied the rest of the packet in the doorway just in front of her, then sat hugging her knees and staring over the gardens, searching for a little black figure.

Amy and Lily had meant to be totally silent, so as not to scare away the kitten, but they couldn't resist chatting. They were deep in a discussion of exactly why Luke Armstrong in Mrs Dale's class was so mean, when Amy suddenly clutched Lily's arm.

"Look!" she ordered, in a hissing whisper.

"Oh!" Lily gave a little squeak of excitement. "Is that her?"

"I think so." Amy leaned out to look further along the fence, where a black shadow was clambering over the ivy branches. "Yes, it's her! Oh, I hope she can smell the cat biscuits."

Scrambling through the leaves, her paws slipping on the thin branches, the kitten certainly could. She was terribly hungry. Charlie was still stealing all her food, and no one seemed to notice – Sarah was always busy, and Mrs Jones wasn't very well and was spending most of her time resting in her chair. Quite often she had Charlie sitting on her now, and she would stroke him, while the kitten watched miserably from under the sofa, or peeping out from under the bookcase.

But now she could smell something tangy and lovely, and her stomach was making little rumbling noises. She trotted eagerly along the fence.

Oh, the smell was getting even stronger and better.

The kitten stopped suddenly, and wobbled on the fence. She was there – the girl from yesterday! And there was another one with her. The kitten watched them warily.

Then the girl she'd seen before held out a little packet, and tipped something out of it, and the kitten knew that was where the wonderful smell was coming from. The tip of her little pink tongue stuck out, she was so hungry.

Amy couldn't help giggling. The kitten was so cute, with her tongue just poking out like that. It made her look really silly.

The kitten put her front paws up on the tree branch, and the girls exchanged excited glances. Then she jumped all the way up, and found the first cat treat. She crunched it up in seconds, and scampered forwards, sniffing for more. When she got to the end of the branch, after about six more treats, she stopped and looked anxiously at Amy and Lily. She could see – and smell – the big pile of treats just in front of them.

Amy sighed. "Perhaps she's too frightened to come closer," she whispered.

Suddenly, the kitten sprung up on to

the tree house ladder, and Amy and Lily held their breath. Then, keeping one eye on the girls, she started to gobble up the treats from the doorway.

When they were all gone, she licked the place where they'd been, then looked up hopefully.

"She's still hungry!" Amy said. "Let's open another packet."

Lily shook her head. "No way. She'll be sick. A whole packet's loads more than she should have, anyway!"

Amy nodded. Then she held out one hand, very slowly, to the kitten, who was staring at her seriously. Amy scratched her gently behind the ears, and she half-closed her eyes with pleasure.

"Hello, Misty," Amy whispered.

Chapter Five

The kitten sat there a little nervously, still ready to run, as Amy stroked her and then Lily joined in too.

"Isn't she beautiful?" Amy said proudly.

"The prettiest kitten I've ever seen – except Stella," Lily added, out of loyalty. "Oh, Amy, she's started purring!"

She had. Amy had just found the exact itchy spot behind her left ear, and the kitten had her eyes closed, and a tiny little throaty purr was making Amy's hand buzz.

"Tea, girls!"

The kitten's eyes shot open. She leaped off the ladder and raced back along the branch, jumping down on to the fence and disappearing away.

"Bye, Misty!" Amy called after her quietly. "Why did Mum have to pick just then to call?" she complained to Lily, as they scrambled down from the tree house. "I think Misty might even have let us pick her up."

Lily nodded. "She was definitely friendly. But you're right, she is much too thin. When I stroked her I could feel her ribs. She needs a nice owner to feed her properly."

The kitten obviously agreed. She came back to the tree house the next afternoon at the same time, and Amy opened one of the tins of cat food she'd bought. She put it in an old plastic bowl she'd borrowed from the kitchen cupboard, and sat in the doorway of the tree house, watching Misty gobble it down. Misty let Amy stroke her again, too, and even put her paws on Amy's leg, as though she was considering climbing into her lap.

"Are you going out to the tree house again?" Mum asked. "It's raining, though! I didn't realize you loved it that much."

"It's my best present ever!" Amy giggled, a little guiltily. She *did* love the tree house, but that wasn't the main reason she was spending so much time out there. Every afternoon that week, as soon as she got home, she'd rushed straight there to look out for Misty.

She threw on her hoodie over her uniform and went out to the tree house. The ladder was slippery from the rain so she climbed up slowly, peering out along the fence for a little kitten. But no kitten came running to see her today. She sighed. Maybe Misty was sheltering from the rain somewhere.

She stood up and pulled open the tree house door, planning to sit and read on the beanbag, while keeping an eye out for Misty through the window.

But the beanbag was already occupied.

A little kitten – her fur shiny and spiky from the rain – was curled up on it, fast asleep.

Now that she had discovered that the tree house had a soft, comfortable place to sleep, and that Amy would come and feed her, Misty spent most of her days there, even though she still went back to Mrs Jones to sleep at night. She had climbed in through the half-open window that first time to get out of the rain, and Amy hadn't seemed to mind. In fact, she'd looked really pleased, and spent ages stroking her. The window was always open a little way now, so that she could get in, and there would always be a little bowl of cat crunchies or something else delicious waiting for her.

"I don't know if I'm imagining it, but I think you're looking plumper,"

Amy told the kitten lovingly, a week after she'd first found her inside the tree house. She stroked the little black tummy, as the kitten lay sleepily in her lap. "Are you getting fatter, Misty?"

"Prrrrp." The kitten purred, and yawned. Then she snuggled up on Amy's lap, feeling more at home than she had for a long time.

Amy stroked her gently, wishing Misty was really hers. "Stay here, puss," she murmured. "This is your tree house now too." But it was getting dark now and Amy knew she'd have to head inside soon, and leave the kitten all alone.

"Amy! Your tea's getting cold!" came her mum's voice, from just below the tree house.

Amy jumped and so did Misty, springing off her lap.

She could hear her mum climbing up the ladder. Panicking, Amy dropped her hoodie top over Misty. She couldn't let the secret out now – not when Misty felt almost hers. Mum would never let her keep a kitten.

Amy's mum poked her head through the doorway. "I've been calling you for ages!"

"Sorry!" Amy got up quickly and went over to her mum, hoping she wouldn't see the wriggling hoodie behind her. She followed her down the ladder.

Misty edged her way out from under the top, shaking her fur crossly. Why had Amy done that?

She slunk over to the tree house door and watched Amy going up the garden towards the house. Misty slipped out along the branch, and jumped down on to the fence, then into Amy's garden. Keeping her distance, she followed Amy, trotting after her. But just as she reached the house, Amy closed the door.

Misty stood outside it sadly. She wished she could follow Amy into the house. It looked warm and friendly.

There was a big magnolia tree, growing close to the kitchen window, and Misty scrambled up the trunk to a branch, then jumped on to the window sill. She could see Amy, and two other people, laughing and eating.

The food smelled delicious. She mewed, hoping that Amy would see her and let her in. But the man sitting closest to the window was the one who stood up and came to look.

"It's a cat!" He laughed. "A little black kitten. Come and see, Amy."

Amy jumped as she saw Misty, accidentally knocking her glass of juice off the table. It smashed on the floor, and the woman got up with a sigh.

Misty leaped back on to the branch, hiding in the gathering darkness, and watching as they cleared up the mess. She wished she was in there with them, but Amy had seemed upset to see her and she didn't know why. Misty watched for a while, until Amy disappeared and the lights went off. Then she pattered sadly down the garden and back up into the tree house. But this time she didn't sleep on the beanbag. She curled up on the hoodie top instead. It smelled of Amy.

"Mum came up to the tree house and nearly saw Misty last night!" Amy told Lily before school on Friday morning. "I had to throw my hoodie on top of her, poor thing! And then she was suddenly there at the window, and Dad saw her!" She sighed. "It's fun having a secret kitten, but I wish I didn't have to hide her all the time. It would be so nice to be able to take her inside, too. I'd love her to sleep on my bed, like Stella does with you."

"It is nice," Lily admitted. "She keeps my toes toasty. Do you think your mum and dad really wouldn't let you keep her?"

Amy shook her head thoughtfully. "I just don't know. I've begged for a kitten for so long – if they were going to let me have one, wouldn't they have given in by now? I can't see them changing their minds."

"But she's so cute!"

"Maybe I should tell them all about Misty. But what if they make me take her to a cat shelter?" Amy shuddered at the thought.

Even so, she couldn't stop imagining how lovely it would be to curl up and sleep with her own little kitten. She just had to think of a way…

"This is brilliant!" Lily said excitedly, as she laid out her sleeping bag on the floor of the tree house. "I'm so glad Mum agreed I could stay over. Do you really think Misty will come and sleep with us too?"

"I think she spends the night here sometimes now. I tried brushing all the cat hairs off the beanbag last night, and there were more this morning. So she must have been here…"

Amy had come up with the sleepover plan at school, and the girls had begged their mums to let them do it that Saturday. Lily's mum had been a bit worried that they would be cold, but she'd agreed in the end, when Lily reminded her about the special sleeping bags they'd bought to go camping. She even had a spare one for Amy!

"This is even better than camping! Oh, I do hope Misty comes," Lily said excitedly, as she clambered into her sleeping bag.

Amy nodded, glancing over at the window from her sleeping bag. It was too dark to see much – especially a black kitten. Misty had spent the afternoon in the tree house, but she'd run off when Amy started to move things around to get ready for the sleepover.

They chatted for ages by the light of their torches, but they kept yawning as it grew later and later.

"I don't think she's going to come," Amy said sadly, when she looked at her watch and discovered it was ten o'clock.

"Never mind." Lily gave her a hug. "It's a brilliant sleepover anyway. Maybe we'll see her in the morning."

Amy nodded, but she did feel disappointed. And as Lily yawned more and more, and then drifted off to sleep, she felt lonely too. The wind was blowing and she could hear the creak of the branches. It seemed to shake the tree house more at night, although she didn't see why it would. Amy lay there with her torch making a circle on the ceiling, worrying about Misty.

Where was she on this chilly night?
Was someone looking after her?

A sudden thud made her yelp with
fright, and she swung her torch round.
The beam caught a pair of glowing
green eyes, staring at her in surprise.

"Misty! You came!"

Purring delightedly, the kitten raced across the boards to leap on to Amy's sleeping bag, padding at it eagerly with her determined little paws.

Amy lay down again, and yawned. "I'm so glad you're here," she murmured.

Misty curled up next to Amy's shoulder, half inside the sleeping bag. It was wonderfully warm. She was very glad she was there, too.

Amy stroked Misty gently, and soon the pair of them were fast asleep.

Chapter Six

"Oh, Amy, she's here!"

Amy blinked sleepily, and looked over at Lily, who was sitting up in her sleeping bag. There was a warm, furry weight on her chest, and Amy remembered her late night visitor. Misty had stayed all night!

"She turned up a little while after you went to sleep." Amy suddenly sat up, making Misty squeak. "Lily, what time is it? My mum! She said she'd bring us our breakfast in the morning."

Lily's eyes widened. "It feels like we slept quite late." She wriggled over to the door and opened it. "Oh no, she's coming down the garden! With toast!"

"I don't care if she's got toast! What are we going to do?"

But they were both sleepy and giggly with excitement about Misty, and all Amy could think of was to pull her sleeping bag up over the kitten. Which Misty didn't like. She wriggled about indignantly, and just as Amy's mum appeared at the top of the ladder, she poked her head back out.

"Hello, girls! Did you sleep well?"
Amy's mum smiled at them. "I thought
you might be hungry." Then she noticed
Misty, and her eyes widened. "Amy, is
that a cat?"

"It's a kitten," Amy told her, cuddling
Misty close.

"Where on earth has it come from?" her mother asked, sounding confused.

"I found her," Amy said defensively. "She's a stray. I've been looking after her."

"But she must belong to someone. Oh, Amy, I think we need to speak to your dad about this. Come back to the house, right now."

Amy climbed awkwardly down the ladder, with Misty still snuggled up against her pyjamas. Misty was shivering, as if she could tell that something was wrong.

Amy's dad was drinking some tea at the table, and looked up in surprise as he spotted Amy holding Misty.

"Amy, isn't that the kitten who was at the window the other day?" he said, getting up to take a closer look.

Misty hissed nervously, as this big man suddenly loomed over her.

"Sorry, kitty. I didn't mean to scare you. She's a sweet little thing, isn't she?"

"But whose sweet little thing, that's the point!" Amy's mum said.

"I don't think Misty belongs to anyone, Mrs Griffiths," Lily put in.

"She's got a name? Amy, you've named her?" Amy's mum stared at them suspiciously. "This isn't just a one-off thing, is it? How long have you been keeping this kitten in your tree house?"

"I haven't been keeping her there. She just came! I first saw her a couple of weeks ago. Just after my birthday. But I don't know how often she sleeps there."

Mum turned to Lily. "All that cat food that you bought! Was that for this kitten?" she demanded.

"Ye-es," Lily admitted, looking guilty.

Mum sighed. "Amy, it's not up to you to feed somebody else's cat! We'll never get rid of her now. Not if you've been feeding her. We need to find the kitten's owner."

"She doesn't have an owner!" Amy protested.

"She must do," her mum said firmly.

"Honestly, she doesn't. She's a stray. She really doesn't belong to anyone. She doesn't even have a collar. And look how thin she is!" Amy paused and looked at Misty. "Well, she isn't now, but that's only because I've been feeding her. She was so skinny, Mum! Ask Lily."

Amy's mum sank down into a chair. "I know you two are in this together," she snapped. "I can't believe you've both been hiding someone else's kitten!"

"Sorry, Mrs Griffiths…" Lily muttered, and Amy put an arm round her, feeling upset. She hadn't meant to get her friend into trouble.

Amy's dad pulled up a chair and took a sip of his tea. "OK. Let's not get upset," he said. "Sit down, girls, and tell us what happened with the kitten."

Amy sat down next to her dad. She looked up at Mum, determined to make her understand. "Misty was really nervous at first. It took ages before she'd let me pick her up. She was really scared. Even if she did have an owner, they haven't looked after her properly."

Misty put her paws on the table, and sniffed hopefully at Dad's tea.

Dad laughed. "She looks hungry.

Shall I give her some milk? Since Amy's already been feeding her, it can't make that much difference."

Amy's mum only sighed, but Amy shook her head. "No, Dad. Cats aren't supposed to drink milk. It gives them a stomach upset. You can give her some water, though. And I could go and get one of her tins from the tree house, if you like?"

Misty mewed hopefully, and Amy's dad nodded. "She knows what you just said. Go on then."

When Amy and Lily came back, Misty was sitting on her dad's lap.

"Dad! I didn't know you liked cats!"

"She was pretty determined." He shrugged. But he was smiling, and he stroked Misty's head very gently, as though he knew exactly how to handle a kitten.

Amy watched, wide-eyed. Mum and Dad had always been so firm about her not having a cat that she'd thought they didn't like them. But Dad looked really happy having Misty on his knee. Amy stared at him hopefully, and then exchanged a thoughtful look with Lily.

Just then, Misty jumped lightly off Amy's dad's lap, stepped delicately around the table to her mum, and sat staring pleadingly up at her, her sparkling green eyes looking as big as saucers.

"She's a charmer!" Amy's dad laughed. "She wants to stay."

"Stay! We can't keep her! I can't believe you're giving in!" Amy's mum protested. "Yes, she is cute, but we said Amy was too young for a pet."

"She's been looking after this one quite well so far," Amy's dad pointed out. "I didn't know cats shouldn't have milk. And this is a very sweet little cat." Misty mewed hopefully at Amy's mum.

"We'd better feed her, anyway," Mum said, shaking her head. "She's obviously hungry."

Amy lifted Misty down from the table and placed her on the floor, while her mum took down an old bowl. Mum opened the tin of cat food and started to empty it out. Purring, Misty butted her head against her leg, making Mum laugh with surprise.

Mum shook her head. "I never thought I'd say this, but all right.

You can keep her here – for the moment. If we find out she actually belongs to someone else, she goes straight back! And I'm going to ring the vet, and check no one's asked about a lost kitten. All right?"

Amy threw her arms around her mum. "Yes. But she doesn't have an owner, I'm sure." She then looked down at the kitten, who was tucking into the food greedily. "This is your new home, Misty!"

Chapter Seven

Over the next few days, even Amy's mum got used to the idea of having a cat. Misty was so sweet, and very well-behaved. Amy's mum had been worried about her making messes in the house, but Amy's dad went out and bought a litter tray, and Misty soon showed that she was beautifully house trained.

"I don't think she can have been born feral," Amy's mum said, tickling Misty under the chin. "She's so friendly. I'm still worried she's somebody's pet."

Amy folded her arms and frowned. "Well, it was somebody who didn't love her as much as we do!" She sighed. "OK, OK, Mum. I promise. We'll give her back, if anyone says they've lost her." But she was certain they wouldn't.

Misty and Amy still spent a lot of time in the tree house. It was Misty's favourite place, and Amy loved curling up there with her. But once Misty had proved she could use the litter tray, she was allowed anywhere in the house, too. She loved exploring – the house was full of warm, comfortable places.

And Amy's dad was very good to sit on. She was even allowed to sleep on Amy's bed, since she hated being shut in the kitchen. They had tried it on her first night in the house, but Misty had mewed frantically, and in the end Amy's mum had given in. Now she slept snuggled up with Amy, or sometimes blissfully curled on Amy's toes.

Amy spent the last of her birthday money buying her toys, and a collar – a pink one that looked beautiful against her black fur.

Misty could still remember her old home with Mrs Jones, but she knew she belonged to Amy now.

Mrs Jones sat in her armchair, staring out at the front garden, and stroking Charlie. But she was frowning. "It's been a week since I've seen Jet now," she murmured to the Siamese cat. "I hadn't realized, because she was only popping in and out even before. But she hasn't even been back for her food." She looked down at Charlie, worriedly. "I have to say, Charlie, you're a bit heavier than you used to be. Have you been eating Jet's meals?" She pushed him gently off her lap, and stood up, leaning on her stick. Slowly, she walked into the kitchen, with Charlie trotting after her.

"Sarah, when did you last see Jet?" said Mrs Jones, easing herself on to a kitchen chair.

Her daughter looked surprised. "Oh. I don't know, Mum." She glanced over at the cat food bowls, both of which were empty. "Well, she's eaten her breakfast, so she must have been here this morning, although I didn't actually see her." She smiled as Charlie wove around her ankles. "It's a pity we can't ask him!"

"Hmm." Mrs Jones frowned. "I don't think we need to ask him. It's clear exactly who's been eating Jet's food. Look how much plumper he is!"

Sarah shook her head. "Oh no. He wouldn't!"

"Sarah, I haven't seen Jet for a week. And before then she was so flighty and scared that I'd only see her here and there for a second. I think Charlie frightened her away."

"Charlie's not like that, really…" But Sarah was looking a little worried.

"It isn't his fault," said Mrs Jones. "This is his house, after all. But we have to find Jet. I should've realized what was going on, but those new pills Dr Jackson gave me made me so tired. Poor Jet! She must be starving by now.

She doesn't know the area at all... She might've got lost or she could even have been run over." Mrs Jones's voice wobbled at the thought.

Sarah came over and put her arm comfortingly around her mother. "Don't worry, Mum, we'll find Jet. I'm sure she can't have gone far."

One afternoon, a fortnight after their sleepover, Amy and Lily were walking back from school, chatting away as their mums followed behind.

"Dad's going to put in a cat flap this weekend," Amy told her friend happily.

But Lily didn't reply. Amy looked round and realized that Lily wasn't actually there. She'd stopped and was looking up at something stuck to the lamp post they'd just passed.

Amy went back to see what Lily was staring at. "What is it? Oh no…"

It was a poster, with a photo of a small kitten, and the words: "LOST. Jet, a black kitten. Please check sheds and garages in case she has been trapped inside. Contact Mrs Sylvia Jones if you have seen our cat." Underneath there was a phone number and an address.

Amy stared at the poster numbly. "Do you – do you think it's Misty?" she whispered to Lily.

"It looks ever so like her," Lily admitted sadly. "And Rose Tree Close is only round the corner from you, isn't it?"

Tears welled up in Amy's eyes. "I don't want to give her back," she muttered. "It isn't fair. Misty doesn't love this Mrs Jones, whoever she is. She can't do, or she wouldn't have come to live with us. And think how thin Misty was when we first saw her – she mustn't have looked after her properly!"

Lily nodded. "What are you going to do?"

Amy looked up at the poster. "I could just pretend I haven't seen it. That Mrs Jones doesn't deserve to have Misty back – I wouldn't feel guilty." Then she gazed at the photo of Misty again. "Well, only a little bit…"

She glanced along the road. Her mum and Lily's had nearly caught them up. She could just tear down the poster, then Mum would never know… But as her mum approached Amy could see that she was holding another copy that she must have taken from somewhere further down the street.

"Oh, Amy. You've seen it too. I'm so sorry, but it looks like Misty has a home after all."

"But how do we know it's her?" Amy whispered.

"She does look very similar," Mum said gently.

"She didn't like her old home, or she wouldn't have run away. She's ours now. Dad was even going to put in a cat flap!"

"I know, Amy. But someone's missing her – this Mrs Jones—"

"She doesn't deserve a kitten!" Amy sniffed, and Lily squeezed her hand.

"We have to take her back," said Mum. "Remember, it was our deal."

Amy was silent for a moment. There was nothing she could say. "I know. But I still think it's wrong."

Back home, Misty wasn't in the house, running to the door with welcoming mews, like she usually did.

"Maybe she's in the tree house," Amy suggested. But a little seed of hope was growing inside her. If she couldn't find Misty, she wouldn't have to give her back, would she?

Amy ran out into the garden, and climbed up to the tree house, but it was empty. She sat down on the beanbag. It felt warm, as though Misty might have been curled up there until a moment ago. "Oh, Misty, I wish I'd kept you a secret," she whispered. "Please don't come!"

But then she heard a familiar thud on the boards of the tree house, as Misty jumped from the branch. The tears spilled down Amy's cheeks, as the kitten ran to her, leaping into her lap.

Misty rubbed her head lovingly

against Amy's arm, and then stood up with her paws on Amy's shoulder, and licked the wet tear trails with her rough little tongue.

"That tickles!" Amy half-laughed, half-sobbed. She picked her up gently. "Sorry, Misty, we have to go and find Mum." Amy carried her down from the tree house and across the garden. Misty purred in her arms, so happily. She was such a different kitten from the nervous little creature Amy had first seen. It felt so wrong to take her back!

"Oh, you found her!" Mum came over to stroke Misty, as Amy opened the kitchen door. "Please don't cry, Amy." But she looked close to crying herself, as she gave Amy a hug. "I don't want to give her back either, but we have to. You know we do. Look, shall we wait until tomorrow? So you can have tonight to say goodbye?"

Amy shook her head. "No. That would be worse. We should go now. Come on, Mum, please, let's just get it over with."

"All right. I'll call the number on the poster. Rose Tree Close isn't far. We can just carry her there, can't we?"

Amy nodded, and sat down at the table with Misty, half-listening as Mum explained to someone on the

347

phone that they'd found their missing kitten. With shaking fingers, Amy started to take off Misty's pink collar. Misty wasn't even Misty any more! She had another name.

"They're really glad to know she's safe," Mum told her gently. "I said we'd bring her round." She grabbed her bag, and they set out, Amy with Misty held tightly in her arms as they walked down their street and along another road, to the little turning that was Rose Tree Close.

Misty looked around her curiously, wondering what was happening. Amy had never carried her outside like this before. Then, all of a sudden, her ears went back flat against her head, as she recognized where they were going.

Why was Amy bringing her *here*? She struggled in Amy's arms and mewed with fright as they walked down the path.

"Oh, Mum, she doesn't want to!" Amy protested, but her mum had already rung the doorbell.

The door opened, and an old lady stood there, staring at them in delight.

"Jet! It really is her! Oh, thank you so much for finding her!"

Amy only just stopped herself from shouting, "No, her name's Misty!" Instead, she stared at the brooch on the old lady's cardigan, which was a little silver cat, with green glass eyes.

"Come in, please! Oh, Jet, where have you been?" Mrs Jones stroked Misty, and Misty actually relaxed and purred, and let the old lady take her from Amy.

Amy felt the tears starting to burn the backs of her eyes again. This really was Misty's owner. It was true. Her little cat belonged to someone else.

Chapter Eight

Misty felt very confused. She was back with Mrs Jones, but Amy was there too. She wasn't sure what was happening. Mrs Jones had Charlie now, so why had Amy brought her here? But it was so nice to have Mrs Jones holding her again. She rubbed herself against the old lady's cheek lovingly.

Mrs Jones led them into the sitting

room, and sat down with Misty on her lap. "Where did you find her?" she asked, smiling at them so gratefully that Amy felt guilty.

"She came into Amy's tree house," her mum explained. "We did ask around, but no one seemed to have lost a kitten. She's actually been with us a couple of weeks. I'm sorry, you must have been so worried."

Mrs Jones nodded. "I was terrified that she'd got lost or had even been run over. I've only just moved here, you see, to live with my daughter, so Jet doesn't know the area very well." She scratched Misty behind the ears, and the little cat stretched her paws out blissfully. "She kept wandering off – we hardly saw her – and then she disappeared. I thought she'd gone too far and got lost."

Mum gave Amy a look, and Amy stared at the carpet, feeling miserable and guilty. Mrs Jones had hardly seen her because Amy had been tempting her away. She'd been so stupid! Mum had been right – she really had stolen someone else's cat.

"Amy looked after her very well," her mum said, giving Amy a hug. "We'd always thought she was too young for a pet, but we've changed our minds after watching her with your cat. We're definitely going to get a kitten of our own. I mean it," she added to Amy in a whisper. "We're so proud of you."

There was a scuffling noise at the door, and Misty suddenly tensed up. She had forgotten! It had been beautifully quiet, almost like things used to be, with just Mrs Jones. But now Millie and Dan were home!

"Gran! Gran! Oh! You've got Jet back!" A little boy raced into the room, and tried to grab Misty.

Amy gasped, as she watched Misty cower back against Mrs Jones. A little girl came running in after him, and tried to pull her brother away so she could reach the kitten too.

"Gently, Dan! Millie, be careful! You'll frighten her," Mrs Jones cried. The children stopped shoving as their mum came in. "These are my grandchildren. They've missed her too," Mrs Jones explained to Amy and her mum. "And this is my daughter, Sarah."

Sarah was smiling delightedly. "I'm so glad you've found her. We've all been so worried."

Amy looked anxiously at Misty – or Jet, she supposed she ought to call her now. She was pressed against Mrs Jones, her ears twitching with fright. Amy thought the children were loud, so she couldn't imagine how a kitten felt.

"We'd better go – leave you all to settle down," Amy's mum said.

"Please, let me have your number – I'd like to call and let you know how Jet is. I'm really so grateful." Mrs Jones stood up, with Jet held against her shoulder, and led them out into the hallway. "My goodness! Jet, what is it?"

The kitten suddenly scrabbled her way up Mrs Jones's shoulder, and leaped to the top of a shelf, almost knocking over a vase. Her tail was fluffed up, and her ears were laid back. Charlie was here!

"Oh, you've got another cat!" Amy exclaimed, seeing the sleek Siamese padding along the hallway, staring up at her little Misty.

"Yes, that's Charlie. He belongs to my daughter. He and Jet don't always get along too well. But I'm sure they'll settle down now that she's back."

Watching Misty spitting angrily from her safe spot on the shelf, Amy thought that it didn't look like they got along at all.

"You were very good, Amy," her mum said, as they walked home. "I really did mean it about you getting your own kitten."

"Thanks," Amy whispered. "Not for a while though," she added. She knew she ought to be happy at the idea of her own kitten. But at the moment all she could think of was Misty, scared by those noisy, grabby children, and terrified of that Siamese cat. It made her want to cry. When she'd first seen Misty with Mrs Jones, she'd thought she'd got it all wrong, and Misty did belong with her. But now she wasn't sure. What if that Siamese had been stealing all of Misty's food and that's how the kitten had ended up so thin? She wouldn't be surprised. She was almost sure that Charlie had made Misty run away. And now Amy had made her go back.

Misty raced across the living room, making for her hiding place under the bookshelf. But she couldn't get in! She wriggled frantically, but she'd grown – two weeks of proper food, and she was simply too big to fit into her special safe place. Why had Amy left her here? Was she going to come back? Shaking, she turned back to face Charlie, who was right on her tail. She hissed defiantly, and raked her little claws across his nose. But he was just so big! With one swipe of his long brown paw he sent her rolling over and over across the carpet, and then he jumped on her.

"Honestly! Mum, she's fighting with Charlie already! Stop it! Bad cat!" Sarah tried to pull the two of them apart as they scratched and spat.

Mrs Jones heaved herself up from her chair, and tried to help. "Jet, Jet, come here. Oh, he's hurting her." She waved Charlie away with her walking stick, and leaned down to scoop up the little kitten. "Oh dear…" She sat down again, the kitten a ball of trembling black fur in her arms.

"Charlie hates not being able to use the cat flap, that's why he's being grumpy," Sarah muttered, picking up

Charlie, and holding him as he wriggled and spat at Jet.

"I know, but Jet might run off again, if we let her out. We need to keep her in for now, so she starts thinking of this as her home." Mrs Jones stroked her gently.

Sarah sighed. "We'll just have to keep them apart until they get used to each other."

Mrs Jones looked worriedly down at the kitten, still shaking on her lap.

"Maybe I was wrong to say you'd get along with Charlie… I suppose I was just so pleased to have you back. Poor little Jet. Whatever are we going to do with you two?"

After school a few days later, Amy was up in the tree house lying with her head resting on the beanbag. There were little black hairs on it here and there. She looked up and saw that, sitting on the shelf, there was still one tin of cat food left, that she'd never remembered to bring into the house. It was all she had left of Misty, that and her collar, which was on her bedside table.

Mum kept mentioning the idea of

another kitten, and Lily had bought her a cat magazine, so she could look at what sort of cat she might like. But Amy just couldn't think about it yet. It would feel like betraying Misty – betraying her all over again, because Amy felt sure they had done the wrong thing by taking Misty home. She kept listening out for that telltale thump on the wooden boards that meant Misty was coming back to her, but it never came. She supposed Mrs Jones was keeping Misty shut up so she didn't stray again.

It had been five days. Nearly a week. Perhaps after a week, they'd let Misty go out into the garden? Maybe she'd come walking along the fence again, and Amy could at least stroke her.

That wouldn't do any harm, would it? As long as Amy didn't feed her, no one could say she was trying to tempt her back. Even just seeing her would be enough. All she wanted was to know that Misty was all right.

Mum was calling her for tea. Amy looked hopefully along the fence as she climbed down the ladder, but there was no Misty trotting along to see her.

She sat down at the kitchen table, picking at her pasta and staring at the newspaper ad that Mum had ringed. "Kittens, eight weeks old. Tabby and white." Amy didn't want a tabby and white cat. She wanted a black one. A very particular black one.

"Has Charlie finished his dinner, Sarah? Can we let Jet in?" Mrs Jones was peering round the kitchen door, with Jet in her arms.

Charlie looked up at her and hissed crossly. He hadn't finished, and he didn't want that kitten anywhere near his food.

"Oh, Charlie," Sarah sighed. "They really aren't getting on any better, are they?"

Mrs Jones shook her head. "I'm beginning to wonder if I did the right thing," she admitted, her voice sad. "Maybe I should have let that little girl keep her. You could see she was heartbroken when she brought Jet back."

"But you'd miss her!" Sarah protested.

"Of course I would! But I think she'd be well looked after. And we still have Charlie. He's a lovely boy, he just doesn't like sharing his house…"

Sarah nodded. "Oh, he's finished." She picked up Charlie, and took him over to the door to put him out.

Misty watched as Sarah began to open the door, and her whiskers trembled with sudden excitement. The garden! The fence! And along the fence, just waiting for her, was Amy's garden, and Amy's house, and Amy.

She wriggled frantically, and made the most enormous leap out of Mrs Jones's arms. She shot out of the door before Sarah could even think to shut it.

She was going home.

Amy sighed, and stared down at her homework. She was supposed to be writing about her favourite place, but the only place she could think of was the tree house, with Misty curled up on the beanbag. A sudden scuffling at the kitchen window made her look up.

"Misty!" Dad exclaimed, looking up from the pan he was stirring on the hob.

Amy ran to the door to let her in. She knelt down and swept Misty up into her arms. Misty purred gleefully, rubbing her face against Amy's.

Amy was laughing, and half-crying at the same time. "She came back," she murmured, and Misty licked her hand gently. Amy's dad tickled Misty under the chin, then her mum came over to stroke her, too.

"Mum, do we have to…?" Amy asked miserably. "She's so happy to be here…" She looked pleadingly over at her dad, but he shook his head sadly.

Her mum sighed. "I know. I wish we could just keep her, but it wouldn't be fair. She doesn't belong to us." She picked up the phone.

"Mrs Jones? It's Emily Griffiths here. Yes, I'm afraid we've got Misty again. Sorry, I mean Jet."

Amy sat down on one of the kitchen chairs, and stroked Misty as she watched her mum miserably.

Her dad put a comforting hand on her shoulder. Maybe Mrs Jones was going out, Amy thought. Maybe it wouldn't be a good time to bring Misty back, and they could keep her for just one night. But that would be worse, wouldn't it? She'd never be able to give her up then.

Misty wriggled indignantly as a tear fell on her head, and then another.

"Really?" The note of surprise in her mum's voice made Amy look up. "Well, if you're sure. We'd be delighted."

Amy stared at her, sudden hope making her feel almost sick. She watched her mother put down the phone and turn around, beaming. "That was the first time Misty had been out, Amy. She came straight back to you. Mrs Jones says that she obviously thinks she's your cat now, and it isn't fair to keep her. She's given Misty to you." She hugged them all – Amy and Misty and Dad together. "Well, we promised you a kitten, didn't we?"

"Oh, Mum! Wait a minute." Amy pressed Misty gently into her dad's arms, and dashed upstairs, then raced back down again and into the kitchen, with something pink in her hand.

Carefully, she fastened Misty's collar back on. "You're really ours now. You're here to stay," Amy murmured, taking the kitten from Dad.

Snuggling against Amy's neck, Misty closed her eyes and purred – a tiny, happy noise. She was home!

The
Scruffy
Puppy

From best-selling author
HOLLY WEBB

Bella has always dreamed of getting her very own dog. And Sid, the little puppy with the mad, frizzy ears, has always dreamed of the perfect home.

Sid loves living with Bella, and she adores playing with him. But then Bella's friends start being mean about Sid. Can Bella prove to everyone that there's more to her scruffy puppy than first meets the eye?

The
Brave
Kitten

From best-selling author
HOLLY WEBB

Helena loves helping out at the vet's surgery where her older cousin Lucy works. When they find a young cat who's been injured by a car, they take him straight there. Helena helps to care for the cat she calls Caramel, but when it's time for him to go home, Caramel's owner can't be traced.

Caramel is fed-up with being kept at the surgery and he especially doesn't like the scratchy bandage on his leg. But if no one comes forward to claim him, how will he ever have a place to call home?

The Forgotten Puppy

From best-selling author

HOLLY WEBB

Emi has wanted a dog for as long as she can remember. So when she gets Rina, a little Shiba Inu puppy, Emi wants to take her everywhere. There's just one problem – she has to leave Rina behind on the weekends she spends with Dad.

Rina can't understand why Emi keeps going away! When one of the trips seems longer than usual, she's convinced that Emi has forgotten all about her. Rina sets off to find her owner. But where should she look?

The
Secret
Kitten

From best-selling author
HOLLY WEBB

Moving to a new house and school is hard for Lucy. Then she finds a family of stray kittens in an alleyway, and doesn't feel quite so lonely. She especially loves the shy black-and-white one, and calls her Catkin.

Catkin doesn't like it when the other kittens are taken away. Then Lucy makes her a new home in their greenhouse. But the kitten can't stay there forever. Just how long can Lucy keep Catkin a secret?

A
Home for
Molly

From best-selling author
HOLLY WEBB

Anya has been worried about feeling lonely on holiday with only her baby sister to play with. So she is delighted when she meets some new friends on the beach. And when a gorgeous puppy, Molly, joins in their games it looks like this could be the best summer ever!

It's been such a long time since Molly had an owner. Then she meets Anya and she doesn't feel so alone any more. But will Anya be able to give Molly the home she's been looking for?

Welcome to the world of
HOLLY WEBB!

Holly Webb
Puppies and Kittens

Available for
Apple iPad
and Android
Tablets

Great **games** and
fun puzzles

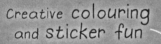

Choose your
perfect pet

Collect all the books on
your very own **bookshelf**

Creative **colouring**
and **sticker fun**

Brand-new short story
by Holly Webb!

HOLLY WEBB

Holly Webb started out as a children's book editor, and wrote her first series for the publisher she worked for. She has been writing ever since, with over one hundred books to her name. Holly lives in Berkshire, with her husband and three young sons. Holly's pet cats are always nosying around when she is trying to type on her laptop.

For more information
about Holly Webb visit:

www.holly-webb.com

GOVERNING EUROPE